OF
PARTICLES
DETACHED AND FLOATING

OF
PARTICLES
DETACHED AND FLOATING

A COLLECTION OF SHORT STORIES BY

RYAN RATLIFF

aventine press

Published by Aventine Press
55 East Emerson St.
Chula Vista CA 91911
www.aventinepress.com

ISBN: 978-1-59330-880-3

Printed in the United States of America

TABLE OF CONTENTS

THE AMBLING REMNANTS OF A TRANSMISSION FROM AN UNKNOWN SOURCE

Millions of light years spanned between,
As a vast parting of the Earth and I.

I looked to the world behind.

And as a frigid current seemed to surge through me,
I began to feel the intolerable sense of isolation.

I missed my family; the sight of faces other than my own.
Certain a longing so great comes of more than absence.

It occurred to me; when observed at such formidable distance,
Life; that which I'd led, that which would continue in my absence,

Lost all definition.

A world living, breathing, coursing and dying,
It is no more, that I can see, than a single sphere.

Only when near others did life gain clarity. Purpose.
Meaning cannot be found when merely observing.

And I'd become the observer.

To think that I should never again participate. Strive.
It meant the remainder of my life would be void.

Love and hate; the abstract concepts emblazoning life.
Far and gaining distance. I had left these in a fool's endeavor.

Value. Slipped my grasp.

In the darkness, amidst the swirling masses I'd failed.
No significant discovery. My words becoming silence.

A return to find the blissful waiting with arms open.
Disappeared as a dream I could no longer recall.

I'd succeeded, only, in finding death.

To any who find this; regardless of the means and intentions,
I've only to say farewell and may none of you be so foolish.

Do not follow me.

There is nothing to be found here save the trifling results of
obsession...

And there is nothing worthy of such a loss in definition.

THE SPIRE
(AND ITS SOLE INHABITANT, BRANDON DALE)

I regained consciousness and found myself struggling under a flight deck in the Atlantic Ocean. After managing to free my head above the waves, I began gasping and drawing several hurried and heavy breaths. I could feel a slight sting with each inhale made frigid in the cold night air. I composed myself with great effort and briefly surveyed my surroundings. Between the distracting buffeting of the waves and fierce glow of flames it was difficult to perceive anything with much detail. Besides the flaming wreckage of the commercial airline which departed from Atlanta and the scattered bodies floating in the ocean, I noticed in the orange glare of the flames, the water appeared slick and black in several areas. I identified it instantly as fuel and could see that it was quickly igniting and building into flames. In response to the evident hazards of my surroundings, I swam as quickly as I could in no certain direction; my only thought was to escape the wreckage and the accompanying inferno. The further I withdrew from the flames the darker the sky became, and in the dim moonlight I could not hope to gather any bearings.

After a short period of drifting, I began to see what appeared to be a small measure of land. It was a strange and unlikely sight, but if it meant I could climb out of the burning waters, it was welcomed. As I approached it, I realized it was just a few hundred feet in diameter and had the distinct shape of a perfect circle as if it were a miniature man-made island curiously perched in the middle of the Atlantic Ocean. Without hesitation, I climbed onto the slick and solid surface and for a moment I sat motionless peering back at what remained of my flight to Brussels.

It occurred to me, of course, that I was the only survivor. I heard no screams for help, and what bodies I could see, were floating lifelessly, moving only in synchronicity to the waves of the tepid water as it quickly caught fire. It too occurred to me, that survivor, as a descriptor, was perhaps premature. I couldn't likely survive for any extensive duration sitting stranded upon a small pseudo-island without food or water.

I sat thinking, curiously about the strange surface upon which I found myself and the natural impossibility of such a minute and stationary piece of land located in the middle of the ocean thousands of miles from anything. I concluded that it simply didn't make any sense.

All I could think to do was to wait and watch the flames burn out in the distance. It would be too dangerous to approach the dismembered plane now, but eventually, once the flames subsided, I could search the area. It didn't seem entirely impossible that something, perhaps nourishing or edible at least, could survive the wreck.

After all, I had survived; to what end, remained to be determined.

For a short while I had been fighting the urge to fall asleep; resisting for fear that I may pass out and not wake. I felt healthy enough and could find no severe injuries, but my body and head remained incredibly sore and I could feel a great sense of fatigue. I knew that any such experience could cause shock to the system and reduce the body temperature to fatal levels and the urge to pass out could be a result of such shock. So, I continued to resist, but even knowing this, and against better judgment…

I lay back, watching the star filled night sky peer through small thickets of light clouds. I relaxed some. The sky was serene, as was the ocean, and it begged the question, what caused the wreck? I couldn't really remember details, only the pedantic magazine I was reading, the uncomfortable seat and the tremendous monotony of ticketing, baggage check-in and security. I sat beside the window on the left side of the plane, and the last I saw of the sky peering through that window, I recall it was late afternoon and the sun was starting to set, behind a few scattered clouds…

There was a crash. I knew that much, and a loud, obnoxious ringing, followed by absolute darkness. I could remember nothing else. The crash; the jarring crash…I couldn't think of where it originated, or its cause. Luck, I guessed; my luck anyways. My eyes began to flit and close. I knew I shouldn't fall asleep…But…

I woke up.

It was a morning sky I found myself staring into, and there were no clouds to be seen, and I could hear nothing. No burning, no waves clashing against metal. It was far too eerie. I sat up, and was shocked. I didn't know what to think of it. There was no plane, there were no bodies, no flames; nothing. I was still sitting on the same surface, but with nothing to be seen besides water. In the distance, for miles, there was nothing but water. Maybe the plane sank? The bodies may have as well, or maybe they drifted. Could the plane have drifted?

How far off was it when I fell asleep? Maybe it was nine-hundred or one-thousand feet at the most. I left my secure little dry piece of isolated heaven and slipped into the ocean swimming until it seemed I'd matched the distance I swam to reach the island. I dove down a short distance and looked through the water as best I could and saw nothing. A thought occurred to me; I had no bearings last night, and the plane could have resided in any direction from the round land mass. I could not remember the placement of the moon, relative to myself or the plane. I swam and dove repeating the task for what seemed like an hour and could see nothing, save for the dark depths beneath me. I couldn't even find any wildlife in the ocean or sky.

I returned to the area immediately surrounding what could be my final place of impact and dove down once more. I opened my eyes to the seawater and let the blur lift until I could see the base of the stone island. It wasn't an island at all; it was more like a pillar or a great spire. It was narrower at the water surface and grew increasingly broader for what appeared to be thousands of feet, possibly miles, into the dark depths until it could no longer be visible.

I returned to the surface and climbed back onto the spire top with a feeling of desperation and sickness. In the daylight, I could better examine my provisional residence. It was an inexplicably level surface, covered entirely with evenly distributed moss.

I pleaded with God for several minutes. I swore away every vice and sin, if I could only see my wife again, or at the very least, live through this experience, somehow. Maybe, someone could find me; another plane, or a ship. It wouldn't be long before I'd be praying for anything; pirates, or even sharks. The endless sky and ocean surrounding me was numbing. It wouldn't be long at all, and I'd be praying for anything to change.

After several hours, I had memorized the exact location of the sun in relation to my position and the spire. With my belt buckle, I etched into the surface, carving through what appeared to be moss, at each edge developing a rudimentary compass depicting the north, south, east and west points on the circular flat, stone spire crest. In the areas where I had scraped the moss and etched into the stone, I could see its color beneath. It was a beautiful golden marble. I used my finger and polished the "north", rubbing until it shined with a brilliance competing that of the sun. I did the same with the east, west and south. I was incredibly bored, but also very fascinated by my strange new home. Temporary, as I'd hoped it to be.

I thought about the peculiarity of the moss, in that I was surrounded by ocean, and moss should not grow in or around saltwater. In curiosity, boredom and possibly even hunger, I forced my hand beneath the growth and retrieved a palm full of the mossy compound. I examined it closely; it looked very much like moss, vibrant green, pilose and somewhat slick. I raised the mass of growth to my face and could detect an odor which resembled pine, wet with rain. Intermingling, it carried another scent, sweeter, and more similar to sugar cane. Continuing in my trend of thoughtless curiosity, I tasted it. It didn't taste as I had imagined moss, or something similar to moss, would taste; not at all. It was very sweet, with a very mild tartness. It reminded me of the taste of pear, but it dissolved, almost in an instant, as soon as it met my tongue. It had an unusual texture, in those brief moments before it dissipated. It was almost gritty at first, but quickly became incredibly juicy and soft, caressing my tongue as it melted.

With the milky remnants of the once fleshy material still residing in my mouth, I lay back again holding some of the strange fruit-like growth up to the sun. It occurred to me...the more I looked at it, the more it seemed to...move? I drew it close to my eyes and focused my vision, peering as intensely as I could. Trying to make out microscopic details with the naked eye, I could only determine that it was, in fact moving, as if it were one single organism crawling within itself, flexing.

I felt ill again. However, it was worse this time...far worse. I lurched over the southern edge of the stone, and vomited into the ocean. The projected contents of my stomach floated thickly in the water and appeared almost black leaving behind the taste of gasoline and metal. I reached into the vomit and swirled it around some, to ensure that it didn't consist of blood, or worse. It didn't. I couldn't determine exactly what it was though, that I had just regurgitated. It was insulting with its strong odor, which seemed almost toxic; like a hazardous combination of carbon monoxide and sulfur. I quickly moved my arm back and forth through the water to help the ocean spread and disperse the fluid. I walked a few steps eastward and dipped my arm into the clear water and rinsed it off. Though I knew I shouldn't, with the current taste on my tongue driving me crazy, I reached into the ocean and drew to my mouth a swig of the disgusting saltwater. It was better than the previous taste which could only be likened to the taste of disease or cancer, or what one could only imagine these tastes to be. I spit out the saltwater, and considered for a moment that drinking it may bring death quicker. At this point it seemed I had little to lose.

So I thought about death, maybe trying to drown myself, or strangle myself with my belt, but I was fooling myself and knew I couldn't do it. They were hopeless, my current affairs, but maybe things could change. It seemed a freak occurrence that brought me here, maybe only for lack of more knowledge regarding the crash, but it could also be a freak occurrence that saves me.

I stayed in the position, stretched over the southern edge of the stone with my left arm dangling over the ocean. Again, I fell asleep.

I woke up to see the sun rising. However, according to the etchings in the spire, which no longer appeared to be accurate, the sun was rising in the south; almost due south. I couldn't understand it. The spire was stationary, near as I could tell. Could it have rotated? Exasperated with the thought, I placed my head in my hands for a moment. It must have been some time I had spent sleeping as I could feel the nearly one inch of hair now jutting from my face. I couldn't know for sure, but if I had to guess I'd say at least a week of growth was now found gracing my face. Impossible! I couldn't have slept so long without being disturbed, not to mention my lack of thirst or hunger. Honestly, I felt refreshed, as if I was in good health. I left the comfort of my hands and stood, looking up into the sky. It was teeming with small clouds and as the breeze gently wisped by, it carried with it countless flocks of gulls. I peered down into the ocean and it appeared to have changed in opacity. It had become very clear and pristine in its color and it was almost as if this vicinity of ocean had become shallow.

I could not believe how refreshed I felt. I felt as though I was coursing with energy and vigor. With a sudden burst of energy, I jumped into the ocean. I opened my eyes under the water, and could see clearly, as if there were no water at all. I followed the spire down for what seemed like several minutes holding my breath. I watched as the water surrounding me was flooded with schools of multiple fish species. These thinned as I travelled deeper. The ocean grew darker as I continued to greater depths and I still could not begin to fathom just how tall the spire must have been. The water appeared almost shallow from the surface, but it certainly wasn't so and after the passing of another few minutes I realized my depths and could finally feel my natural need for air. I spun in place and swam quickly towards the surface. Reemerging, I took a large, deep and strangely sweet-tasting breath. It seemed unlikely anyone should have the ability to hold their breath for such a long period. I was not exactly sure of the time, but I would certainly wager that it would have broken records.

Lying upon the spire again, I stretched my legs, digging up the mossy material as I pushed them out. The moss seemed loose and almost graying in color, as if it were decaying. The spire itself glowed brightly in the sun in the increasingly exposed areas. The surface seemed brighter, far brighter, than I recall the day, or perhaps week, before. I cleared a small area of moss and threw the growth into the ocean. As soon as it hit the surface of the water, it dissolved almost completely and in an instantaneous flash of bright, glowing green, it expelled hundreds of particles floating into the sky, disappearing. The unique sight resembled nothing I had ever seen in nature. It was remarkable, and doubly depressing, in that I may be the only person who would ever see it, and I would likely take the memory to the depths with me.

Would I ever see my wife, Annecy, or children, Jake and Pearl again? What must they be thinking right now of their father? Would they have received the news that I hadn't made it to Brussels? Certainly, a missing flight with no survivors would be news worthy, and after all, I was not a known survivor.

My sister, Mary Dawson, who had provided my invitation to Brussels along with the all too common push to do something I'd had second thoughts about, wouldn't find me at the Royal Belgian Institute of Natural Sciences. Jean would have already introduced his discovery, the Ishango Bone, and I would likely be over a week late to the unveiling. To be sure, the Paleolithic tally stick may very well have paled in comparison to the spire now securing my place above the ocean. Being made by man, entirely of some gold and marbled stone, stretching miles into the ocean, my current homestead could likely be a historical milestone. If ever I return, I could possibly introduce an even greater discovery than Jean's bone. Mary would be absolutely floored, if she could see this, but how incredibly unlikely it would be that anyone else should see me or The Spire again. I didn't believe any soul would ever see what I had seen, and I was still struggling with the certainty that I was actually seeing it. I really shouldn't see any such thing. None of it; the spire, the moss should not exist. And if it is real, and I'm not just floating on some piece of wreckage, delirious and starving, then it too, is moving, or shifting, because the oceans and skies around me have been changing somehow, with each passing day.

My eyes had been closed with these reflecting thoughts. I opened them, looking directly into the sun. I focused away and allowed my vision to restore. Standing, I stared down at the golden surface, beaming through the decaying foliage lifting in small swatches with the wind and dissolving into bright flashes, like thousands of luminescent emeralds. I wasn't delirious. I couldn't have created this in my head, implausible, though its existence may be. I've just never been that imaginative.

I thought of an experiment I could conduct. I ripped my belt from my waist and leaned over the eastern edge of the ocean. With my belt buckle in hand, I carved a line into the spire indicating the current water level. As I did not know the date, I simply carved a one followed by a dash and two, for noon. This would be indicative of each quarter of each day etched just above the corresponding line. I figured each following day would proceed in ascending numerals. Whether or not measuring the variation of the water levels would yield any results was yet unclear. However, I was curious to determine if there was an existing constant in the daily fluctuations of the water levels. At the very least, I would have developed a more interesting and possibly productive way to pass the time.

Standing up again, I executed some simple stretches intended to help limber my body. Following these stretches, I performed jumping-jacks, ran in place and dropped to the floor to finish with sit-ups and push-ups. I used to do these stretches and exercises every morning before leaving to the office where I would sit sedentary at a desk for ten hours of the day. Of course, it occurred to me that I should have no energy to perform these exercises considering the amount of time that must have passed since I'd last eaten. I performed well and felt as if I'd expended no energy; as though I was brimming with energy, and could feel no fatigue whatsoever. After completing my typically exhausting exercise routine, I didn't even break a sweat.

Looking towards the west, I realized time had passed and that it was late afternoon, nearing dusk. The waves had receded slightly and I marked their third quarter location, roughly four inches below my previous line. I realized I would need to find some way to pass time further, until nightfall when I would make the final mark and sleep until morning; provided I would greet the next day.

I decided to take a short swim. After winding my belt around my hand in a way that left the buckle in the palm of my hand, I leapt from the western edge and performed an expert dive into the ocean with great ease. Over this short period, I had developed an expertise in not only diving, but swimming and water acrobatics as well. I performed several rolls and flips and pushed myself deeper and deeper, testing my limits before needing to return to the surface for air. Once I had reached the point I knew would spare me just enough energy and air with which to reach the surface, I used the buckle and etched a mark into the side of the spire. I quickly raced back to the surface and gasped.

After I had returned to a normal and steady breathing pattern, I drew myself closer to the spire and using my index finger from the mid-knuckle to the tip as rough representation of an inch I marked down one inch from the top of the spire. I then drew in a deep breath and kicked back under the surface and continued marking, travelling down one inch at a time from the spires surface until I had finally reached about an eight of the depth I'd first marked. I returned to the surface, steadied my breathing and repeated the process several times, continuing from the previous mark and adding inch after inch. Finally, I'd reached the first mark indicating my absolute depth and had also reached the point at which, I could hardly hold my breath. I could feel the pressure growing in my lungs and them almost heaving inside me in response.

I rushed towards the surface at a greater speed than I could recall ever being capable. This was reached in what was likely record time and I pulled myself back onto the spire with the dwindling energy still afforded me. After laying on the surface for a moment to rest and gather my thoughts, I calculated the amount of feet I had travelled into the depths. I'd counted 15,049 inches, which would equate to 1,254 feet. I smiled with my head swimming in an almost delirious, but euphoric state, partially caused by the struggle to return to the surface, but also because this was by any definition an absolutely superhuman depth. It was I, of all people, who had performed the feat. It was getting dark and I could see the moon beaming brightly over me, and so I made my last mark of the day.

The two-one mark was considerably deeper than one-four which had risen to about one inch from the surface of the spire. The two-one had fallen to nearly twenty-seven inches below. The new morning brought yet another shift in position, given that the sun then appeared to be rising in the north. Unless the ocean was sinking and the earth breaking its billion year-old rotation, the spire was most certainly on the move, somehow; I just couldn't figure that part out.

The spire—my primary stability was shifting. If my only solid, my only form of familiarity could remain so alien to me then it would leave me questioning everything and slipping from the grips of the tangible.

I jumped—again.

With my mind thoroughly cleared of any introspective thought, too resoundingly difficult to comprehend, I had decided upon another menial task. This time, rather than diving and testing my depths, I thought I might as well try distance. However, foreseeing the issue of swimming out too far and not being able to find and return to my only form of even remote concreteness, I decided against the idea. Instead, I would swim laps around the spire and attempt to calculate the distance based upon the spires circumference. I swam towards the edge of the spire, removed my belt and laid it along the radius with the buckle and a small part of the belt itself falling over the edge only slightly, this would be my lap marker.

Estimating the diameter of the spire to be about three-hundred feet and adding in the twelve or so feet, I would buffer between myself and the spire's edge, I figured a lap would entail approximately nine-hundred and eighty feet. I had no knowledge of any swimming records in terms of distance travelled, but assumed if I broke any records, I would likely never be able to brag about it anyway. Considering that should I one day return to the blessed abundance of land, rather than monotonous ocean, I could never prove any of this had actually occurred. Regardless of any of these truths, I swam.

I kept swimming, in a mind-numbing repetition of circles completing lap after lap, only stopping to make my quarterly marks of water levels and to spend a few moments calculating distance. It soon grew dark and I pulled in towards the edge of spire, calculating for a moment, the distance travelled, I made a mental note and made the final mark of the day. Two-four, at twenty-three inches remained very close to two-three and two-two, which were twenty-four and twenty-six inches respectively.

I considered turning in for the night, for what, to the best of my apparently inaccurate estimates in time, could be a day, week or month spent sleeping. Rather, I thought, I should remain awake, and witness the mythical turn from night to day and all that it had appeared to bring with eyes wide open. This could also lend itself to my continuation of a record-breaking swimming distance and my constant battle to maintain corporeality.

With that, I returned to my starting position and continued. Throughout the night, I swam non-stop. I found no need to mark the spire levels as I considered that it would break my routine, having not recorded this at night before. I did keep the spire in my peripheral sight and from what I could see, the water levels hardly shifted, leading me to believe a great deal of time must have been passing while I slept.

Morning came, and I made the mark of three-one, at a minor shift of twenty-seven inches throughout the entire night. I kept swimming, making my mark which at three-three had climbed to about fifteen inches. It was difficult to mark very accurately as the ocean had picked up some turbulence. Three-four finally came at a water level of eleven inches. And I kept swimming, again tirelessly, through the night.

By the time of four-two, seven inches, I was through with swimming; I could feel the fatigue finally burdening my physique. With a few minutes spent in calculation, I had figured the distance in miles to be close to one-hundred and eighty-two. It was likely a record, and definitely should have cost me my life.

Having climbed back onto the spire's surface, I lay down, stretching out my legs and arms. Staring at the clouds I could feel the need for rest haunting and weighing on my eyelids. I struggled to remain awake as I needed to finish the day and mark the remaining quarters, but closing my eyes, I declared my defeat.

Startled awake by the sound of thunder and the growing dampness, I quickly rose to my feet, and frantically looked around to survey my surroundings. Waves, that were barely choppy before that moment when I had succumbed to the temptation of slumber, had become fierce and devastating. Smashing back into the ocean, crashing into other waves, then growing rapidly taller only to collapse onto themselves with awe-striking ferocity, the waves seemed to dance around the spire taunting me and perhaps warning me. It would only be a matter of time before one should contact the surface, and sweep me away into the undertow. As I stood in tumultuous fear, I could see and feel the water rising beyond the spire's surface and climbing up my legs.

I looked down to confirm, the darkness was growing so quickly I could hardly see deeper than the water's surface. I could just make out the shape of the tattered remains of my shoes, but I could no longer see the spire. I was still standing, I knew it was there, but it was no longer visible. The strange structure that had become my homestead, which had encompassed my life for the seemingly vast amount of time beyond which I could hardly remember, was vanishing quickly.

I had no time to consider the reality of the situation. I had to act; to do something, regardless of the outcome. I had to swim and fight the overpowering currents, if only to battle the inevitable. I swam in the direction I had perceived to be north based on my recollection of the spire's surface etchings. I fought with every ounce of strength to push forward. I made so little progress and only managed to travel further into whichever direction the storm and sea wanted to carry my futile form. I kept forcing my hands and arms through the embittered waves and kicked my feet to the quickest and fiercest of my abilities. On a rising motion I turned my head and saw to my left, a behemoth of a wave; so colossal it blotted out my view of everything beyond it. I took in a deep breath and dove, going deeper and deeper, hoping I could avoid the force of the crash. Being nowhere near quick enough, I could feel the full force of the impact; quick, bludgeoning and beyond anything I could have imagined. I felt myself slipping away and within mere seconds, everything bled away into darkness.

I opened my eyes. A great task as if my eyelids were weighted with lead. They were swollen, I knew the feeling. They ached, in correspondence to the rest of my face, head, and entire body. I felt as if I had been hit by a train. My sight began to focus and sounds began to chime in and register with my eardrums.

So much time needed to pass before I could even fathom my surroundings. There was such a stark contrast to the open and endless ocean where I had only previously found myself struggling against the great fury of the sea. I was on land, dry land that I knew to lie beneath, but I could not see because I was surrounded by walls, a floor and a ceiling.

I was in a hospital room of some kind. It appeared to be simple and meager; like a hospital found in some small and rural countryside village. The sun was beaming through the open window to my left, and I could hear the chirps and whistles of birds. I could still smell the sea in the air, wherever it was I'd found myself, I was on land but still near that revolting sea. I tried to recall what had happened. I must have been knocked out after the wave hit and carried me undertow. It would have been nothing short of luck or a miracle that could have carried me to a shore or ship or whatever it was that managed to bring me ashore.

A young man, assumingly the nurse dedicated to my survival, entered my room and appeared to be shocked to find me awake. I must have looked like hell, or death. He began to speak to me, but I could not understand the language. I tried to speak in my own dialect, but couldn't, instead I listened as he rattled through a few more words. I could place it; it was Portuguese. I tried again and was able to muster out with great effort, "Ingles". He understood, adjusted the dressings on my arm and leg, which apparently sustained some minor damage, and shortly left the room. Even though I ached, to the best that I could feel, nothing seemed to be broken. I felt thirsty and incredibly hungry. I no longer garnered that inexplicable energy and resilience I experienced on the spire. I supposed this only meant that I was returning to reality, to the world that I knew before all of this took place.

The young man returned with an attractive, older Portuguese woman who looked very similar to the boy, and they exchanged a few words, all of which were completely foreign, save for the word I had offered earlier which I knew to mean "English". She must have been the resident translator. Turning to face me, she moved in closer and spoke softly with an amazing accent made all the more wonderful, in that they were the first few words I'd heard and understood in such a long time.

"Hello sir, my name is Dr. Rosa Caldeira. My son has informed me that you speak English. Is this correct?" She was completely fluent.

So I mustered with some effort, "Yes, I'm American. Unfortunately, I don't speak Portuguese. Please, may I have some water? I don't think I've ever been this thirsty."

My throat and mouth suffered in a stiff aridity with each word.

"Certainly. May I ask your name? When you were discovered on the beach, no identification was found. I suppose it was lucky you even had your clothes. They were mere threads."

She spoke laughingly, with an attempt to comfort me.

If she only knew what it meant to me; to be anywhere with people, and a bed to lie upon. It was indescribable. It felt like a millennia since I'd last felt linen or cotton that didn't belong to the tortured remains of my own clothes. To call it comfort would be an understatement. I drank the cool water from the glass she'd offered me and nearly choked myself trying to guzzle it down.

"Easy, I'm sure you're very thirsty, but no need to come this far only to choke yourself to death."

She retrieved my glass and propped my head.

"Brandon Dale, I...I was on a flight coming from Atlanta. I was headed to Brussels when our plane crashed into the Atlantic."

"When was this? If you can recall..."

She seemed to be struggling with the same thought embattling my mind. Far too much time must have passed since the plane crash.

"I...The flight left on a Monday. It was September 3rd...I had no way of telling time after the crash. I tried to keep track of the time with the sun, but it seemed the earth was working against me."

I added the last sentiment in hopes to help spur her to tell me the current date and possibly alleviate any thoughts that I was a completely demented or psychotic.

"That plane crash in the Atlantic was reported on the news worldwide. They had to dive to find the wreckage and the black box. They reported no survivors. I think it was caused by an engine malfunction. Something that was affecting that particular model. It was in the news for several weeks. A recall was issued for an entire fleet of airline models, but Mr. Dale...that was over three months ago."

Three months she said. I couldn't believe it. I had guessed a few weeks, but months? No, even then, in my lax state of mind, months seemed impossible.

"Months? I know you must think I'm crazy, but it was that very plane crash and somehow I survived. That much, if only that much, I know for certain."

I wanted to continue, but was finding it difficult to judge her sentiments and reactions. If she had already figured me mad, there would be no sense in fueling the fire.

"I don't think you're crazy Mr. Dale. Any extreme cases of shock or taxing situations can result in temporary delirium. Perhaps, Mr. Dale, you had seen this news cast before you'd become stranded. It's possible that such a catastrophic event, even when witnessed second hand through a news report, could carry a large significance in your mind that after some shock has occurred, only it remains in your memory." Not crazy but delirious. The only qualifier separating the two is temporary. But it wasn't the case. It wasn't shock affecting my memory, I had experienced everything first-hand, and she didn't know the half of it.

Still, I thought for moment to continue, and attesting to my own sanity even after describing the impossible spire and the un-heard-of healing properties of an unusual moss growing in the middle of nowhere. The word impossible kept coming up, and I knew she could never believe it or trust me enough to accept that I was being sincere...and not delusional.

"Maybe it would be best if you continued with your rest. I'm sure the details will come back to you as your memory returns. As I said, it's quite possible the experience has left you in a state of shock. In the meantime, do you have any family we can speak with? We can then make arrangements to have you sent home once you have recuperated." I appreciated all of the help, regardless of her questioning my story, and the thought of seeing my family again was almost too much to bear.

"Thank you very much. Please call my wife, Annecy Eunice Dale of Baltimore, Maryland. Tell her I'm alright and that I love her. She'll contact my sister; Mary Dawson, who can handle wiring the funds for the flight arrangements and covering my medical expenses. I truly appreciate all of the help." It occurred to me that she would speak to Annecy, and with my story verified, I could maybe continue, and explain all that happened without my sanity being in question.

I was dead.

The thought occurred to me. If the flight had no survivors, then as far as Annecy, the kids, Mary, the office, the government— as far as anyone back home would be concerned, I was dead. Would Annecy be able to believe a doctor calling from Portugal three months after the crash?

"Wait. She may not believe the call. Would it be possible for me to speak with her? So she knows I'm alright, I can leave the hospital, if need be. Honestly, I must do this. I really think it's the only way." I arose quickly out of bed in order to show my return-ing constitution and stamina. I stumbled slightly, but I must have proved my point.

"I generally would not recommend that you return to your feet so soon, but I do agree that it would be best if you made the phone call, Mr. Dale. I must tend to another patient, but my son should be returning soon if you wouldn't mind waiting for him. He will show you to the phone. Goodbye for now, Mr. Dale." Dr. Caldeira left the room after I returned the farewell and my thanks.

I followed the nurse through a series of long sterile and de-pressing halls, passing rooms all of which contained people who were likely in far worse condition than me. Eventually I was led into what must have been the main office of the hospital and Juan, as I learned to be the young man's name, after a few staff members we continued past referred to him as such, gestured to the large dial phone mounted to the wall.

Before I could retrieve the handset, Juan stopped me quickly interjecting in an apologetic tone, "uno momento, eu devo discar."

This must have just struck his memory. He dialed a couple of numbers and then referred to a directory posted by the phone and dialed several more.

I dialed Annecy and waited with a greater angst and lack of patience than I had ever felt. It was almost unbearable waiting to hear her voice again.

It rang four times and then I heard, "Hello?"

It felt like it had been a century since I last heard that voice; it was Annecy.

"Annecy?" In that moment, it was a struggle to even speak her name, with my eyes welling up in tears.

"Br...who...who is this?" She was flustered and had obviously been caught. It meant she recognized my voice, but she couldn't possibly understand the circumstance—yet.

"It's me Annecy. It's Brandon. I survived the crash, I...I can't tell you how great it is to hear your voi—"

She cut me off, "Brandon, it can't be. They said there were no survivors. Oh Brandon, is it really you? How?" She too, was struggling.

"I barely survived...I should say, it's a long story. I made it away from the wreckage and managed to stay alive drifting at sea, I'm not even sure how, but...Well, eventually I guess I was swept under and knocked unconscious. I actually just woke up maybe an hour ago in some hospital in Portugal. I'm not even exactly sure where I am. I only knew I needed to speak with you immediately. I just want to get home and see you and the kids again."

In split seconds, dozens of possible replies from my wife had raced through my mind, ranging from the negative, like perhaps she'd moved on, to the hopeful, in which, she says she misses me, can't wait for my return, and immediately phones Mary, arranges the flights and I return home where everything returns to normal. I couldn't decide which, if any of these hypotheticals, were most realistic.

"I...Brandon, I just...It really is you. Please, just come home, whatever you need me to do. Just come home. I love you." Her words were almost indecipherable through the sobbing and had I not been hanging on to every one of them. I might have missed the uneasiness hiding in her voice. My heart sank. I could only imagine what it could mean. I wanted to try to draw it out, but I thought better of it, and decided returning to Baltimore would be my greatest obligation.

Still, I tried to draw it out. "I love you too Annecy. I'll find the doctor who's been translating for me and find out the best way to go about this and call back, but in the meantime, if you could call Mary at the office and let her know what's happened. I'll need her to wire some funds and arrange the flight."

I waited several seconds as the phone silence grew more and more malicious. I couldn't handle it.

"Annecy, what's wrong?" I was blunt, but managed to caress my words and keep them tender, if only to distract from my shear panic.

"Brandon...Brent took over the business, after it was declared you had...I've been living off the money left to me in the will..." She was worried about the money; that was it. I almost laughed with relief.

"I left the business to Brent in my will. I guess I didn't think about that...It's really going to be different isn't it. But I'm sure I can work it all out with Brent when I return. There's no need to even worry about that. Just call Mary and let her know what's going on, and I'll be back to see you as soon as I can. I can't wait to hold you in my arms again." I'd thought I was successful in reassuring her.

However, she replied grimly, "Mary passed away. She was on the same flight as you and wanted to surprise you. She'd worked it out so you wouldn't know, putting you in first class and she... It was my idea, I knew you'd be uneasy going alone, we'd had it all planned out..."

Mary was dead; my sister, the one who had raised me after our parents were killed in the fire. The one who insisted I start my data systems business when everyone, even Annecy had little faith in its success. The one who had convinced her husband, Brent, to invest in what he had seen as an incredible risk. My confidence, my success, even meeting Annecy, I owed it all to her. And that was the uneasiness; that was the dread in Annecy's voice. She's gone.

"Oh God I...I can't believe it. Annecy, I...Mary...I need to get home." I trailed off in thought with my head against the wall, leaning only very loosely, clutching the phone to my ear.

"I'm so sorry Brandon, I didn't want to tell you this and have you thinking about it the entire time until you returned, but, I couldn't lie to you and pretend..."

"No, Annecy, I know. I need to know. And that's not true. I'll be thinking of you, and the kids...I'll speak with the doctor and call Brent myself. I should speak with him. Annecy I love you and miss you terribly. I'll see you soon."

"I love you too. I can't wait to see you again."

I hung up the phone and I turned to head to the door as Dr. Caldeira entered the office.

We had a short conversation and she informed me that the hospital was located in Colares, Portugal and the nearest non-regional airport would be over ninety kilometers away. I would need to arrange for a driver to pick me up, on top of everything else. I was certainly building up expenses, but it didn't matter. I needed to get home, and soon.

With the doctor's permission, I used the phone once more, dialing Brent Dawson. The conversation would prove to be a difficult one.

"Hello, you have reached the office of Brent Dawson of Dale Data Systems, Brent speaking." He sounded different. Embittered and aged. I could only imagine what the past few months were like for him.

"Brent...it's Brandon." Likely not the best introduction, but I was at a loss with how to proceed.

"...Excuse me? Is this some sort of a joke? I've no time for this." The tone of Brent's voice ensured me that the conversation would, by no means, come easy.

"Listen, please don't hang up. It is Brandon. I survived the plane wreck, by some sort of fluke of nature I survived. I'm not even sure myself how it all happened. I don't know that I could explain it, but I'm in Colares, Portugal. I must've been carried by the waves, I…"

With great excitement in his voice, Brent interjected, "Brandon…It really is you, how could this be possible, but…are you alone? Were you the only one who…"

I knew where he was leading the conversation and interrupted, "I'm sorry Brent. I spoke with Annecy…I am the only survivor. I watched the wreckage burn that night, and I…I saw no others. Mary…I didn't see her."

I began weeping. I could hear him do the same and it seemed as if several minutes passed before either of us could regain the conversation.

It was Brent.

"I'm sorry Brandon. This is all very terrible. It's a blessing that you survived. I'm sure you must be incredibly homesick. And we all need to see each other again. Annecy, most certainly, needs you home. Please, just—anything you need. I'll handle it. And maybe… if you made it, it seems to be less foolish to hold out hope. It's a miracle indeed to even hear from you Brandon. Three months…"

He trailed off, retreating into thought. If my surviving could boost Brent's faith in Mary's survival, I certainly had no place in shaking it, even if I didn't share the confidence.

The conversation proceeded for several minutes and throughout I began to realize just how deeply Brent felt for my sister. She would leave a tremendous void; it seemed, in both of our lives. As trying as the entire experience had become, the conversation was very sobering.

Fortunately however, I did not have to spend too much time alone. After I spoke with Brent, everything moved rather rapidly. He had made the flight arrangements and scheduled for my arrival in Baltimore less than a week from that day. Time progressed slowest while in the hospital as I waited anxiously for the time for my departure.

That day, I was driven to the airport in an incredibly cramped European car. To add to my discomfort, I was dreading the flight. I had not wanted to fly, but knew it would be the quickest way, and even with the experiences both of us had recently endured in regards to flight, Brent assured me it would be the safest method of travel. The faulty structural design that was responsible for the crash and been recalled from all of the defective airliners. Needless to say, I had my doubts.

Shortly after arriving at the airport, I retreated to the restroom to vomit. After boarding the plane I took a couple of the sleeping pills Dr. Caldeira had given to me. I figured for the second time, if the plane went down, at least, I would die in my sleep.

It didn't happen. I'd returned home that day to hug and kiss my loving wife and children for the first time in what seemed like decades. Brent was also there to greet me. We all had dinner and some long conversations after I had read the children stories in bed, as I had been yearning to have the chance to do the entire flight home.

Brent had begun the arduous task of reviving me on paper. I would once again take control of the company, with Brent as my partner. I'd also confessed to the both of my closest loved ones, of my experience on the spire. They reacted at first with a similar belief that I must have been delusional, but a long night of my exhausting details and great conviction, would leave them believing that something utterly phenomenal had happened to me. Ultimately, we agreed it shouldn't have much consequence. We should try to ensure that life would progress much the same as it had before, with our main concerns being our loved ones. In truth, I was glad for it.

That night, I'd spent the accrued passion and desire of several deserted, lonely months with my wife. It was a fitting end to an amazing day, but floating loosely around the edges of my euphoric daze were the insistent reminders of death and the spire.

Another few months had passed, again with incredible speed, as I quickly regained a daily rhythm in a life similar to that which I'd lived before the spire. Before long, I'd become accustomed once again to a comfortable routine. However, I'd found my free time and free thought to be encompassed with something entirely different from the normal activities and hobbies, with which I had usually associated myself.

Annecy would sometimes refer to it as an obsession.

In spite of this and perhaps in spite of our agreement, I began researching early history and archeology. I'd spend several hours of every day in the library combing through analogues, encyclopedias, and every form of research material I could get my hands on. I'd return home, oftentimes only to continue this habit in my study, devouring late hours of the night in search for the one thing I needed to understand; the spire.

One such night had come; I had found myself in my study, tirelessly searching through paragraphs and pictures, when I'd come upon a book of ancient mythologies in my own personal library. In this book, I had found the strange description of an ancient tower, known as "The Tower of Ndesindaera".

A tribe of men known as the Vorynes, believed to have been eliminated around 1450 B.C., in Europe, now what would be Norway. They followed a number unique pagan beliefs, to which this apparently mythological tower belonged. The tower description and the accompanying illustration were inexplicably similar to the spire. A monolithic and brightly metallic, almost golden tower was believed to travel from sea to sea and ocean to ocean endlessly moving along upon thousands of small legs hoisting the tower's countrywide base which crawled slowly on the seafloor. The top of the spire was coated with a thick green growth referred to as the "Ndesin Daera" or "Life Moss". This plant was said to give unending life to any who eat it. I thought about this for a brief moment, the thought that I'd consumed a plant that gave eternal life. It would explain my survival, but not very well, and certainly not in any believable manner that I could ever hope to use to convince others. This was not to mention the entire mythology surrounding the moss, which had become more disconcerting and even frightening when I continued.

The Vorynes believed this moss existed for a very specific reason; the same reason which explained why they had the custom of sending all of their departed in small boats out to sea. The tower existed for the dead. As a sort of divine transportation system, it would appear only for the dead, who would eat the moss and await their ascension into the afterlife. This would come when the tower reached the heavenly shores of "Storendahld". This did not happen for all however; some cursed and evil souls would remain, forever alone on their own personal tower drifting from sea to sea in a form of purgatory. They would wait for the day that would never come, only able to leave the horrid reality through dreams— dreams that would show them what they could never have, what they did have, and lastly, constant and irrevocable dreams of what they had done to bring about the curse. I closed the book at that point. The thought was terrible. The details rang too true for comfort, but I'd decided against the possibility of its truth. They were mere myths and nothing more. I had, after all, discovered the book in my own library, which meant that at some point in time, like all of the other books I'd owned, I'd read through it. So the possibility entered, that I could have read the book before, and the recollections of the story had entered my mind while I was lost at sea. Maybe I had been delusional, and something else entirely had happened.

No. It was far too real.

I spent that night in bed, beside my Annecy, battling numerous conflicting thoughts, when I'd arrived at one strong enough to settle and bypass all others. I thought about the last part mentioned in the book; about the dreams of what evils one had done to land themselves on an eternally drifting tower—*my evils*. I had led a pretty innocent life, with very few regrets. The only regret I could think of now, is not being more perceptive, maybe just enough to save Mary. Could that have been possible?

I then thought more deeply about my sister. She had always been there to protect me and shield me, to help me along and encourage me to become more than what I'd thought I could be. To become someone else; someone better. My impression, as far back as I could remember, was that she was my guiding hand. Losing her was almost like losing all ambition; all drive. I owed my life, as it was and as it always had been, to her. She had always pushed me to do everything. Even growing up I think I listened to her more than our parents. I guess it was only natural for her to take over raising me after our parents died.

When we were younger and we had survived that fire, even it was because of her. Rather, I suppose, it was because of us together; we had saved each other, in efforts to save ourselves from the fate of our parents.

For a brief moment I drifted through the memories lost in my mind and I stopped upon the image of my sister and me standing side-by-side and hand-in-hand before our house as it roared in flames and I could hear the screams of those still trapped within. When our parents were killed...

I woke up having drifted off to sleep beside Annecy. I opened my eyes and found myself staring at an all too familiar bright blue sky. I could hear waves lapping and crashing in the distance, and at my back, I could feel the cold hard surface.

I could feel The Spire.

FALL OF THE SYNTHETIC EMPIRE

We will be stifled in thought and voices silent.
These flowing waters will recede,
And our coveted will end with their bodies spent,
Beneath the rubble we'll concede.

Entombed as relics in the ashes of our past,
With faces telling of our days.
Yet will the decadence in ruin be steadfast,
Just to blemish a future gaze.

If we are spirits then we've nothing left to haunt,
In broken, rusted, shiftless forms.
As stagnate waters breed infection of our font,
Let our bereft become dust storms.

Selling every fruit born of our wretched seed,
Of ourselves made contaminate.
We as modified amassed productions still bleed.
To corruptions we abdicate.

Crooked teeth gnawing rifts into these burning skies.
Natures of things devour self.
Binding us to the concrete with contorted ties,
Is the end, in and of itself.

NO MEANS TO LIGHT THE WAY

In a long forgotten earthen tomb, I find myself trapped and alone with no voices to be heard, but the echoes of my own. Mimicking and mocking me in this dismal isolation. Yet sometimes, I do hear foreign sounds; sounds not self-produced. Somehow.

Those whispers, cries...screams.

In the dark, that I simply shut my eyes or open them, to continue with no perceivable means to light the way; I can see them. The creatures from a world unknown; from a realm unseen; from a dimension unparalleled.

In and out of the mind's eye, in both the physical and mental realms. Whether they are corporeal or ethereal, they exist, untethered to and uninhibited by the possible. They haunt me in my solitude.

Speaking no words, they instead quake out sounds of dread, malice and sorrow. The sounds grow in volume as they grow closer. My heart retreats deep inside and sinks into the pit of my stomach and I feel as if I could collapse and never awaken. Even so, I find myself paralyzed in a moment of terrible shock as one of the beings reveals itself to me.

At first a single, gleaming, but murky yellow eye nestled in the tip of a strange fleshy protuberance makes itself visible at a level which implies the creature's great height. After but few moments, from beneath the veneer of darkness, the being proceeds to grow even more visible as it draws near; until I can decipher every unnerving detail of the entire horrific face.

Another eye finds itself on the opposite side of the head and is barely visible, tucked beneath a large swelling of tissue. The mouth, almost centered within the face and surrounded by decaying flesh, is perched between two abhorrent tubes, appearing as something similar to intestinal tracts that jut from the face and travel far down into the darkness below the head. Within the mouth, as small as it appears to be, I catch sight of what must be hundreds of long and slender teeth. In the interior bands of tissue, many more subcutaneous teeth can be seen. Accompanying these identifiable features are several small, but nonetheless remarkable holes pocketing the terrible face on either side.

I force my eyelids shut, as tight as I can summon the strength to manage with my state of near petrifaction.

Still, the creature remains.

In fact, it continues to draw near. I open my eyes realizing the futility of the endeavor and watch, motionlessly in silence.

The abomination proceeds slowly, through the darkness growing towards me.

I gather my strength and turn around. Running in the dark at a desperate speed, I can see nothing and have no frame of reference to let me know how much distance I've traveled.

I fear however, that no distance has grown between myself and the horrid beings at chase behind me. I dare not stop, nor look back. The only option is to continue forward for as long as my weary body will carry me.

It seems like an eternity is spent in the chase before my footing betrays me and I slip, falling to my hands and knees. Every instinct screams in demand that I arise and continue.

I cannot.

In moments, I can feel an insurmountable pain as what must be thousands of teeth enter my abdomen and chest with instantaneous, uninhibited force. I can't fight back. I can't struggle as the mouths now surrounding me, gnaw, gnash and pull in opposing directions. The strange feeling of numbed paralysis is sporadically interrupted with moments of shear, indescribable agony as my body gives itself to the forces taking it from me.

To the extent that I can identify my own remains, I am split into four sections. Yet in at least one, the one still connected to my brain, I remain conscious. In brief, ambiguous glimpses, I can see the other parts of me, as they feed the beasts of the unknown.

I close my eyes once more. Perhaps by some divine mercy, I am allowed to leave this realm of consciousness, and the abominations are no longer visible.

I awake from this nightmare in my home; to the sight of my wife lying beside me. I can hear the subtle footsteps of my son as he rushes to our room to startle us awake with shrieks of laughter. This day is envisioned in such great detail as are several years of life following. I almost allow myself to become fooled. But I know the truth. It is fantasy. Grand and lovely, but it is a world conceived of thought, and I know that in moments, my mind will finally be relieved of life and I will leave this fantasy, and with it, the horrible reality.

In mere moments I should pass.

But many moments fade into the past. I no longer feel pain. I feel nothing and hear nothing. I fight an urge to no avail and I open my eyes.

Before me, I see a blessed pasture, backed by a sky so idyllic it seems entirely unreal. Birds sing beautifully in the distance and the scent of lilacs wafts in a caressing breeze.

I should like to stand; maybe remove my shoes and walk barefoot in the soft grass, but I cannot move. I struggle and attempt to expend any kind of energy, but I feel no movement, no appendages, nothing. Attempting to scream I produce no sound. It is as if I am a spectator; a pair of eyes and ears condemned to observe, but serving no other purpose. Surely, it is another fantasy. I close my eyes and open them once more.

Darkness surrounds me.

I hear nothing, but am assaulted with the stench of decay. As if seen by the mind and not the eye, I am made completely aware that I am surrounded by thousands of the atrocities that had previously attacked me. In a vast group, they all stand with attentions thoroughly fixed upon my place. They watch motionless, as if waiting.

If I am now no more than a head; then my head is quickly turned upright and my point of view is rotated until I am peering above me. Here, I see a vast head of bone and feather stretching into a grand beak cleft in twain at its vertical center. A pale white in bone, an obsidian black of feather and a crimson red with viscous gore coursing along the crevices of the skull in the form of thousands of nerves routing the base of the head to its impossible features.

At the endings of these nerves, the head is studded with thousands of black and red eyes and the number of eyes is equaled by a collection of seemingly human teeth, all built upon skull in no conceivable design. No symmetry and no meaning; as if the eyes and teeth were simply allowed to multiply unending upon the massive head.

But as I stare, through no will of my own, I watch as the eyes and teeth detach from the face and float of their own accord, forming countless asynchronous halos orbiting the head. The eyes begin to spin quickly, the teeth begin to vibrate frantically and from this movement, a voice is created in the silence.

In countless sounds too loud and distorted to understand, words are formed. Words, which have not been spoken in eons. Words, which no mortal man has heard and should never hear. Words, which in themselves are pain, sorrow and suffering.

I hear them all. I see it all. Just as quickly as before, my head is spun around again until I see the great collection of beasts once more. Now, they too, are shaking and bellowing in tones that sound of screeches and clacks. The grand collection of the spectacular sights of the abhorrent becomes more than I had ever fathomed a being could bear.

Like any great condemnation worthy of human fear, it is never ending. It hints at an apex, as if leading to something through some ceremony. It never completes, it only repeats these sounds and sights until my memories are lost, swallowed by the repetition and my mind is filled with thoughts dedicated solely to this endless chaos.

If it was glimpses of my previous life I was given, and if I was briefly shown an unattainable heaven, then now it is certain that my fate is that of the accursed.

DYSTOPIC LIGHT

I walk this room's four corners,
Until the process loses meaning,
And I halt for a moment,
Just staring at the ground.

I see the windows fractured light,
As it shines upon the floor,
And I remember a time,
When once this was profound.

It seemed the night was endless,
We laughing through the dreary,
Held back our tears,
As we waited, holding hands.

We knew we couldn't outrun them,
And the laughs were delirious,
With a fear then gaining,
Weighted upon demands.

In moments they would find us,
And we'd find no words to tell them.
Their minds would surely be,
Made up anyway.

We criminals of passion,
Constitute a future,
Of children born,
To see another day.

Somehow we broke the cycle,
As we did lay, that night, together,
Minutes before,
They found us in the dark.

Before our eyes, morning came,
And they dissolved into a past,
From which,
We recovered without a mark.

And now I wait once more,
But this, it is a new day,
And I'm pacing,
Anticipating what it brings.

In a room, you lie adjacent,
I can hear your voice is straining,
But I hear another,
The sound of emergent pings.

The midwife comes to greet me,
Her arms are filled with promise.
I see your face,
Once more, as you arrive.

With hope, we find the morning.
With time, we form a future,
And we remember; for this,
Our past we survived.

A SOLILOQUY
FOR THE MEADOW

When I was a child, my father, mother and I visited a serene and secluded clearing in the small woods not far from our home. A beautiful setting full of wildflowers and buzzing insects my father had chosen after we'd spent some time searching. It was well worth the time expended with great anticipation. Here, we enjoyed the day as a family laughing, playing and delighting in one another's company in ways not readily available to us in those times spent focused upon daily routines.

I remember this joyous occasion not simply for the moments shared in bliss with loved ones, but also for the significant sense of familiarity I recall experiencing while visiting this unique spot for the first time. Though, at the time, it was a scene most certainly new to me, it felt as if I was recalling memories of this unfamiliar location. These memories shared that same ambiguity surrounding the meadow, both strange and familiar, as if they were not my own, or perhaps were mine, but were of times yet to come.

We were not alone, as I recall, and yet in some strange way, I seemed to think we were. There were others; other adults, other boys, a young girl, and a woman. Some shared my young age and some older by several years. But we carried on, with our own company, and they did the same. It seemed the time in that meadow was also for them, equally well spent, with their respective families; their loved ones. To enter this meadow with any but the most benevolent of intentions would've found one entirely out of place. Thus these strangers shared the same smiles, the same laughter, and the same songs as had we. I felt as if I knew them, and they me, though we had not met in any traditional sense.

When the day ended I reflected and puzzled. Though initially perplexed, I was pleased enough with the preceding moments to let them be remembered fondly and with peace of mind.

Time passed as we returned to our lives. That day in the meadow, though not forgotten, became obscured with the haze of time. I retained only those details my mind seemed to insist remain relevant; those that would surface in life's idle moments.

After several years our family grew, by my father's request, with the addition of twins, a boy and a girl, four years younger than I. My mother, initially opposing the adoption as a response to her infertility, eventually warmed to the idea, or merely gave in, as time would reveal to be the more apt explanation.

I did not mind my siblings and our devoted father, a work-at-home artist, greatly enjoyed the added lives. The same could not be said for my mother. Apparently encumbered by the added responsibility, she returned home from her office later and later each night until the late returns halted altogether.

My father tried, dearly, to maintain our shorted family, but the burden resulting in our mother's abandonment had attached itself firmly to the despairing man. His life reached its limit and, by his own hand, ended abruptly.

We found new guardians in my grandparents; our grandparents. I, though young, recognized a need and shared as much of the task of raising my adopted siblings as could be managed with my limited experience.

After my sixth year of school had ended I found the time to fulfill a promise made to the twins and myself. With my sister and brother eagerly in tow, I returned to the meadow. I knew it would be difficult, with the potential to ignite feelings of loss still smoldering within. For the twins, however, it could be as splendid a place, as it once was for me. I'd sincerely hoped it would.

At first, I found it difficult to keep a light heart and a guise of bliss for the twins, but the difficulty subsided and I found myself enjoying the meadow once more. This time was of great need for me, as it was for them, and it reminded me how such a time could be so sorely missed.

Once again, the feeling returned. Confusing as ever, though I recalled my time spent in that meadow as a child, the memory seemed to be one of several. The others, however, were vague and came to me as if they had passed with great loss in definition through the fog of years to come.

Laughing, playing and sharing with my siblings the knowledge shared by my parents in that time too long past, I realized, once more, we were not alone. We shared those meadows with those same families from before, and I recalled having great interest in one particular couple whom I seemed to recognize. They, there with their young son, carried on happily as I watched with joyful tears welling in my eyes. Though they were strange to me then, I somehow felt I knew them well.

That night, we let the bleeding light of the moon cascade freely along our bedroom walls. With a fade into the depths of unconsciousness, I let the day's preceding events take their place among my fondest of memories.

More years progressed since that visit to the forest and my life found trouble once more. Time, not spent in that meadow, seemed to be a curse.

My brother and sister, not being of blood relation, and not being considered financially feasible, were sent to a foster home. In the time to come, we were never allowed the opportunity to become reunited. I remained, more alone than ever, with my grandparents, whom I resented greatly. In this resentment, I might add, they joined my mother.

At age eighteen, I left my grandparents without hesitation. I was eager to begin life anew, as a man with goals to succeed in life where those I resented had failed. My education after high school became precisely focused in etymology. After two years of dorm living and arduous courses I happily met my wife to be. She was a psychology major of fair skin and bright, ever-curling red hair.

Her light blue eyes punctured with ease through the time-tested shielding of apathy and catharsis I had created for myself.

During this courtship, I'd dedicated nearly an entire year granting her all time I'd not previously committed to studies and I was exceedingly glad she did the same. Those numerous moments we'd spent together were splendid in their entirety and I felt free to lose my concerns in her presence.

In a moment of complete comfort a single impulse found an ease in its inception and I allowed myself to commit an act I'd intended from the very moment we met. I invited her to accompany me to the meadow, and she agreed. There, we set a picnic, laughed, danced and sang. With all the meadow seeming to act in harmonious support of our love, I proposed. It was a momentous occasion and, again, the meadow proved to be void of despair. We remained, as an engaged couple, for quite some time in one another's arms. We did so in the company of others, concurrently familiar and strange, all as delighted as we, in each our own wonderful moments spent gladly amongst the beauteous nature.

We shared that night in my bed with her in my arms. The past claimed the day and held it in exaltation, as had I with her, with the memories now accompanying those other too few moments spent in that wondrous place.

Our lives continued in that same blissful charm we'd known in youth. At a relatively early stage in my life I managed to receive tenure from the same school that afforded me the knowledge required to find myself with such a blessing. My wife, equally successful in her young practice as a psychologist, retired shortly after.

We never produced a child having learned I was rendered incapable due to a genetic defect I inherited. Though this discovery was met with initial despair, we remained contented with one another's company.

Considering adoption; I proposed the idea to my wife. She hesitated and before she had the chance to reluctantly agree, I suggested a pet fearing any repetition of my past experiences. It was a reasonable compromise and our adopted beagle found a loving home with us during its fourteen years of life.

With an ardent grace, the years, though greatly cherished and fondly reminisced in turn, passed quickly. At the onset of age eighty-nine, my wife passed before me and again I was alone. Time slowed significantly but I knew my days after her would be short in number. With this in mind, I decided that one last time, and for the first time in solitude, I would return to the meadow.

Among the flowers and the trees still blooming and delighting in this same sunlight now caressing the face of a withered old man, I sprinkle her ashes. I bid her one final and tearful farewell and kiss the petal of a lily, her favorite flower, much like the one that would've found its place just between us in a loving moment far past. I sit as I have sat before with these once puzzling memories now finding themselves enlightened with age. I watch, as I, at once a delighted child, at once a blissful young man, and at once an eager adult share my most treasured moments with the other simultaneous incarnations of myself in this favored meadow where time and the world, in all their adversity, cease to be. Now, I allow myself to pass soundly, knowing that were it not for this place, I would not have survived.

CLOSING TIME

She falls apart around closing time,
Does it again and again,
And picks the pieces up once more,
As the sun cracks its way in.

If her life's some kind of story,
It's one devoid of romance.
She exists in all those moments,
Found without circumstance.

She turns the diner's open sign,
To start yet another day,
Greets all the folks as they pile in,
And watches time waste away.

Thinks if she could leave this town,
Start again somewhere new,
She'd find life's been waiting around,
For her to take her cue.

But the show is always over,
Just before she makes that move.
She turns the sign around again,
Hoping things will improve.

But it's closing time once again,
As she looks back on her day.
The night takes her hope in hand,
And dashes it all away.

And it's closing time once again.
Every day's always the same.
She builds herself up to the end,
Only to back away with shame.

A MOMENT COMMITTED

He had followed her for a few days, working up the courage to pose the question.

She was well aware of this of course; he wasn't exactly subtle. In fact, he was clumsy and his efforts to hide this would often result in exactly the opposite of his intentions.

But when he approached her and requested that they date, she smiled and replied simply, "I will if you can promise me one thing. Should things not work and our time together come to an end, can you promise me that I will be left unchanged, neither better nor worse for the experience?"

He thought for a moment, and then turned away, leaving her. He knew he could promise no such thing.

Months later, he returned to the diner where she had worked and where he had watched from time-to-time in a corner booth. After waiting for nearly an hour for her to arrive, it seemed she was nowhere to be found. Upon asking another waitress about her absence, he discovered she had left the city. This was all he learned.

He had painstakingly prepared a response that he intended to present to her that day. Though on that day he had not had the chance, he vowed to secure these words in his mind should he ever encounter her again.

"It's certain that I cannot promise this, and while I would like to assure you that I would commit myself completely to making our time together perfect, I know that's not the answer you're seeking. So I can only impart what I've learned. A moment in time spent without consequence yields no memory, and when we are left in those inevitable moments of solitude looking back on the life we've led, we would be tormented when recalling no life at all. And so, moments spent in either agony or bliss, they provide our lives, changing as they must. In truth, I am no longer certain that I wish to date you. Instead I have one offer. I can kiss you, or I can slap you. And in this way, when you've time to recall, you will have at least one memory of your life, and I should prefer that memory to be of me."

Sixty-five years passed. He had married, had a son, three grand-kids, and twelve great-grandkids. A full life provided him a mind full of memories. Still, he had made sure to keep room for those words, should fate ever allow him the opportunity to use them.

As it happened, after becoming hospitalized for an ailment which was finally taking its toll, he had found that he shared a room with this woman of his past.

Like him, she was dying. He knew not of what, but he knew, by the looks of her lying in her hospital bed, she would soon suffer his same fate. It was very likely she too, had led a full life; full of memories in which he had hoped she would find peace.

Even so, he had a promise to keep. After slowly climbing out of his bed, he lumbered for minutes until reaching her. Kneeling down beside her, he grasped her hand and as he had rehearsed countless times, he gave his reply.

When finished, she looked to see his worn face and smiled a smile he had not seen in many years. Struggling, she leaned forward and kissed him, explaining, "You are right, and I have lived a life full of memories, both sorrowful in the passing of loved ones and joyous in the moments we'd shared. And these moments were found only after I stopped avoiding them. So I suppose we owe this moment to one another, and maybe it's fitting it be our last."

She closed her eyes as he laid his head beside her, doing the same.

SEA AND SKY

Watching as the day ends.
Looking for amenities,
In the dusk.

Holding the breeze in the palm of a tired hand,
Losing all but sympathy for those fools,
Who always overlook the sky.

A cancer floats in the distance,
Distorting the remaining sunlight,
Hoping to breed along the horizon.

Shadows have never been darker.

Filtered through this day of noise,
The sea becomes pronounced,
Defeating its own restlessness.

As blankets of orange mingle between the waves,
Comforting madness with illusion,
Closed hands and bowing with hidden eyes.

Clasped around knees,
Arms with hair stuttering in the wind,
Pointlessly excited but never to be stifled.

As the sun sets, the night finds itself silent.

Watching below a streetlight,
As pools reveal sky in the pavement.
The moon glows in the caressing mist.

Sky thickening beneath the stars,
As the silence exchanges itself,
With the sound of concrete struck with rain.

A welcome dithers as a flame,
Drowned in the falling chaos,
Lost as trailing smoke in a blanketing fog.

A clear morning reveals the absence.

THE OLD MAN
AND THE MOUNTAIN

"The only source of knowledge is experience."
- Albert Einstein

Long before the schisms formed the continents as we know them now, there were but two pieces of land, surrounded by only one ocean. The mainland, a great continent of forests and deserts, bore many inhabitants, none as formidable and significant as man. The other, a mere island, had but one inhabitant, an old man, known to be ever-existent, beyond the realms of time and uninhibited by death.

Atop the greatest mountain, standing steeper than any on the mainland, this fabled, immortal being lived in quiet solitude awaiting the rare visits from those robust enough to swim through the strong currents dividing the two lands; those with enough endurance to clamber the treacherous cliffs surrounding the small island, and those very same with the required determination, who would finally scale the great mountain. To those few, the old man blessed true knowledge, and though it was simple in its delivery, it provided meaning, fulfillment and reason to any and all things. Those who would seek him need only ask but one question and would receive the answer to all.

So it was that any willing to scale the mountain would return to the mainland, if they sought to return, no longer in question, but utterly at peace and content with absolute fulfillment. Of course, others wished to be privy to this knowledge without performing the arduous task, but it simply could not be shared by mortal man, even by those willing to do so.

As a result, a scheme was shaped and tempered in the spoken throes of unwilling men. One man would carry with him a great length of rope secured at one end to the tallest peak of the mainland, tasked with securing the other end to the mountain of great knowledge. Through the immense power of the falling waters rushing down the face of the mainland's peak, simple machines would be enabled to carry people from the flat mainland plains to the mainland's apex and then be carted across this expansive and carefully woven cable to the mountain of the old man. With this, they believed all would be given easy access to the otherwise rare meaning of all things.

Man after man descended the island mountain, cable in hand, having refused to secure it upon receiving the meaning. It was believed the old man would convince these visitors to not only hold their tongues, but to also refuse to help others to acquire this singular answer. Debates ensued, ideas formed and a decision was finally agreed upon. One man would offer his sacrifice so that all others could be given such access to this knowledge.

Eventually, among the rabble, one such man made the offer and willed himself the suffering of the horrible disfigurement required of the sacrifice. In a ceremony for all to see, the ritual was performed. Long spikes were driven into the volunteer's ears, so that he may not hear, his eyes cauterized shut, so that he may not see, and tongue cleaved clean of his mouth so that he may not speak. He survived and after days of recovery, was sent on his journey, with the cable held firmly in hand. The chosen man swam clumsily through the channel, struggled blindly up the cliff side and ascended the monumental peak with little sense of direction, and guided by an unknown source of determination. Upon his return however, to the shock of the people of unknowing, the rope remained firmly in his grasp. For though blind, he saw the old man, though mute, he posed a question, and with deaf ears, he received the answer.

Again debates ensued, but this time they escalated into battles and years passed before a compromise was met and one idea enacted. An ox, with the rope tied to its neck and secured by bolt to a vast stone weight, would be boated across the sea and guided by man up the mountain. Man may be swayed, but beast would not, and with the man no longer driving the ox, it would by its own volition and lack of strength, stay atop the grand summit with the cable anchored to stone. After a lengthy period had passed, the man returned, and as predicted, the ox remained at the greatest height known to man.

Machines were quickly constructed as promised and in short time, the first five people privileged with the maiden voyage to the mountain left in high spirits. But as they returned, they were sulking; for they saw no old man, they made fruitless inquiries and they heard no great words of an omniscient wisdom. The process was repeated many times with the same unfortunate result. And yet, every so often, one so determined would opt to swim, struggle and scale as had the others before. They would return, fulfilled, knowing the face and hearing the words of the old man.

Despair and resentment plagued the others not willing to seek the meaning. They instead, declared it to be a farce. The words of the unknowing mass resounded in agreement that these supposedly gifted others who spoke of tranquility and blessing that only they had been allowed to attain, were liars and worse, reveled in their facade. So they were strung; all who had made the ascent, hand-to-hand and neck-to-neck and lastly wrapped body under rope around one massive tree in the heart of the mainland. They, with the tree, were set afire, but those who watched with their minds sore in the absence of meaning, numerous they were, saw not one face, of those bound to this burning tree, absent of the expression of bliss.

IN MY PLACE

In my place I'd left a clone,
In hopes that they'd leave me alone.
Instead they chose to seek me out,
And found me in my darkest bout.

I'd wished they'd gone and left me be,
And accepted the simulated me.
To be needed was all I could take,
But to be needed I'd designed the fake.

Without a doubt it would never die,
When certainly someday would I.
And it would do all that they ask,
Make no complaint of any task.

Free to do all that I'd seen fit,
And they'd the equal counterfeit.
Instead they wished to suffer me,
And made short work of my copy.

But maybe it was I who'd died,
And I, the clone, who had survived.
So soon I'll opt to make one more,
And curse it with this living chore.

THE STORY OF THE BLIGHT

I am going to tell you a story; a story I thought worth mentioning. This is a story that will uplift you, and will make you think; so much so that you will not be able to finish your last thought before every thought ricocheting around inside your otherwise empty mind, is converted into a thought regarding this particular story.

This is the story of a boy. I say "boy" to iterate just how demeaned this fellow is, because this fellow would actually is closer to the age of thirty-nine when this story begins. This boy, or fellow, is known as *The Blight*. He stands a not-so-striking two feet and three inches tall. He is the common and shared burden of his town. The Blight is despised and dishonored on a regular basis; roughly every twenty minutes, strictly because of his size. When others come to visit the town, The Blight would usually be stowed away in some tiny cupboard in some small house just outside of town, and just outside of curiosity, never to be acknowledged.

It isn't that he cannot work. He can, and he does, yet he is ridiculed, kicked around and laughed at until he goes home after a very hard day. At home he cries and sobs, secretly to himself, because in a situation like The Blight's, revealing emotions to anyone, means more ridicule, more getting kicked around and more laughs at his personal expense. To be sure, it isn't that he is stupid, he isn't. He is perfectly literate, and can carry on an interesting conversation, if anybody would have it. No, The Blight is The Blight because, and only because, he is very, very small, and is therefore, considered something of which to be ashamed.

At this point, I feel I should let you know that The Blight was much more commonly referred to simply as Blight. Shortly after

he turned four, shortly in this case meaning exactly two days, because that is how long it takes the town to gather a council to
discuss certain matters such as this, the majority of the town, majority meaning ninety-nine point nine percent with the remaining
point one percent being, of course, Blight himself, decided that
someone so unimportant, so unremarkable, and so insignificant
as Blight should never be referred to as '*the*' anything even if it is
'*the*' Blight.

Perhaps I should have mentioned this earlier, but my mind
wanders, and my pen follows. Should you have the desire to retell
this story, maybe you would be so kind as to add this piece of
information to the beginning, and also while you're at it, add that
the town is known as Showver, another bit of information I forgot
to mention earlier.

Now Blight, not *the* Blight, had a secret. A secret that nobody
knew, not even himself, or even those closest to him. These being
his only living relatives; his grandparents, whom, I might add, were
those such loving ones to bless Blight with his seemingly apt name.
Blight would soon discover his secret; his significant, remarkable,
and wholly awe-inspiring secret. One day he returned home to cry,
as he generally did after a hard day of ridicule. Though on this day,
something was different; he decided to cry while sitting on the
stoop just outside the door of his house, rather than laying with his
face wrapped tightly in his pillow on his small bed.

> *One moment. Terribly sorry.*
> *I thought I could hear a cat mewing at my door and figured I*
> *should check to ensure it was just the ever-present madness making*
> *terrible use of my mind.*
> *It was. Thus I will return to the story.*

Shortly after he began crying, shortly this time meaning in a
matter of one half of a second, it began to rain with dark, gray
and bleak clouds covering all the sky above. Blight noticed this
right away and thought to himself in amusement, perhaps the gods

are crying along with me; with this thought he stopped crying and smirked, because though the thought was absurd, it was nonetheless uplifting. I may not need to tell you this, but I will; at the very instant he stopped crying, the dark clouds instantly dissolved and spread away revealing a beautiful bright blue sky with a sun that shone down magnificently and directly upon Blight.

Blight thought deeply for a moment and retreated inside his house; into his small and insignificant bedroom where upon the unremarkable nightstand beside his feeble bed stood a picture frame holding a rendering of his grandparents. He lifted the frame and stared into the image for a few moments and recalled the first time he could remember being referred to by his depressing name and how both his grandparents, whom he sincerely wanted to love with reciprocation, cackled and remarked upon his utter stupidity when he had asked what his name meant. Blight became frustrated and soon enraged when with his flooded by all the thoughts of all the times he had been laughed at and kicked around. The picture frame cracked, snapping inwards with the glass shattering all over the floor. Blight calmed himself quickly, and then returned outside. As soon as he stepped out of the door, he noticed that much of the land immediately surrounding his house was blurring with heated vapors coming from the ground which itself was dead and dry.

Thus Blight, *The* Blight, learned his secret. The secret that had been unknown to him for all of his twenty-seven post-pubescent years, as this remarkable secret had simply not existed until Blight had reached puberty, when all significant personal realizations typically occur. He would have recognized this much earlier, had it not been for his constant self-loathing confinement and an early instilled sense that he should never, ever, succumb to his emotions, except when his face was buried deeply into his pillow for none to see.

Now, there are many choices to make when in The Blight's position, having just discovered that he could control the climate and the atmosphere; *his secret*, as it should now be made obvious to those not closely following.

Two ideas initially occurred to The Blight. He could force himself to become enraged and acquire revenge by terrorizing the town with malicious heat waves that would blister the soul. Of course, he could also show the town his truly amazing talent and win their respect by performing a few kind-hearted demonstrations to their ever-important crops, giving them all the sun and rain they could ever ask for. This second thought carried The Blight to a grand idea; one that, perhaps, wouldn't have come about if he hadn't been surrounded by a town full of such greedy, careless people whose only concern in life seemed to be fortune and honor. His idea was actually fairly simple; he would capitalize on it. The Blight would predict the weather.

> *There it is again.*
> *If you'd be so kind as to pardon me once more.*
> *Nothing.*
> *I should explain that I did once have a cat who insisted he be free to venture, on occasion, into the woods surrounding my home. He would then return and claw and mew at the shut door, wanting to return and likely sleep on the small padded chair I leave untouched in his memory. He actually passed twelve years ago, but not a day goes by that I don't hear him mewing at my door. I suppose I should just ignore it, but somehow I hope for his improbable return.*
> *I have been alone in this house for decade; my cupboards are nearly bare and I am too frail to embark upon a journey to the market.*
> *If he returns, even though it is completely unlikely, I would, at least, have something to eat.*
> *Come to think of it, I believe I did eat him out of desperation.*
> *Yet I am still here, twelve years malnourished. Maybe I'm wrong about the time...*
> *And I am rambling again.*
> *I do apologize and will return to the story.*

The Blight's idea should work perfectly. He could tell others that he predicts the weather will do this or that. They certainly wouldn't believe him at first, but if he made enough accurate predictions, certainly at some point in time it would catch on. It would be inevitable. In regards to the truth of the matter; that he wasn't merely predicting such things, but was actually causing them. It could potentially come to light with dire consequences, but he had no concern. Nobody could possibly find out that his emotions were the cause of the climatic effects, because at this point, due to several years of humiliation forcing him to hide it all, he was nothing short of a master when it came to strictly controlling and of course, hiding how he felt.

The day following the day he realized and formulated his plan, The Blight returned to Showver. He performed his normal duties dealing with the everyday nuisances, all the while telling a random person now and then that tomorrow would bring rain and lots of it.

"You're not only a two-foot tall pile of unremarkable nonsense, but you're foolish to boot. Claiming that you can predict the weather. Pathetic. You're simply feeling sorry for yourself, and desire undeserved attention. Off with you!"

This, among others was, of course, an entirely expected and likely predicted response. Regardless, The Blight continued his day in much the same manner until everybody was sick of his prophesizing and sent him home.

That night, The Blight worked up a depression that could humble even the greatest of depressions. He recalled everything hiding within his memory that could be used to produce self-sympathy. He did so, all through the night and even wrote a despicable and terribly dreary letter to himself with the intention of reading it after waking up very early the next morning, after a night in which he literally cried himself to sleep. He would read the letter and remind himself of how sad and horrible his life had been. It rained. It stormed and muddied up everything. The entire day saw nothing but gray skies. The Blight did not leave the house, and the same went for the entire town. Most thoughts fluctuating throughout the town in response to the boredom of such a dreadful day were of The Blight.

"Nothing to it. Just coincidence. A pathetic pint-sized stain could never be blessed with such ability."

"He was so sure of himself, though…No…No, you're right… Nonsense. Nonsense and mere coincidence."

The following day was bright, warm and could easily fill one with a wholesome lift of the spirits. The Blight was happy; the happiest he had ever been, in fact. He convinced himself things would look up and that shortly, now meaning two days, the town would come around and see him for what he was. Around the town, doing the usual and this time protesting that surely tomorrow would be bright; brighter than the current day, and that there would be no clouds in the sky. The Blight proceeded with high spirits, and of course, if his predictions were accurate, the town would slowly start believing that what was just recently utter nonsense, might bear the semblance of truth.

Another day, another prediction. This time Showver would see a small, light flurry of snow. Significant, as snow had not touched the ground of Showver in roughly fifty years. The prediction came true and everyone, including any remaining doubters, came around and truly believed that this little insignificant speck might truly have something to offer.

In case you are wondering, and I'm sure you are, our dear friend The Blight had concocted a simple method with which to make it snow. He abandoned all form of emotion that day, because, as we all know, emotion is a radiant heat that stems from the soul and of course the lack of any radiant heat means cold, and thus…snow.

But now, I am hungry thinking of that cat. I can remember the taste. Savory with the hint of bittersweet…

I should stay focused upon the story and ignore the pangs of an empty stomach.

I'll continue.

The plan insisted that The Blight continue kindly providing his predictions with enough variance to ensure the town keeps coming back, but with enough sunny days to keep the town happy, at least for one more week. Time flew by and the town quickly began to respect this small man and in due time, he became something of a hero. This meant the time had come for the plan to take its true form; it was time to deny anyone and everyone a prediction without first receiving some form of compensation.

To appease the crowd, rather than coming out and directly demanding some sort of pay in return for his predictions, which would have, undoubtedly, laid waste to the entire plan, he explained to intently listening ears that he has, for quite a while now, helped them out unconditionally with his ever-important predictions. He explained that he merely wondered if it was at all possible that in some cases they could find it in their hearts to help him.

They did.

First they fixed his rotten shack into a proper home. Then they made sure he had food.

Food...Cat...

Clothing and some entertainment helped to keep him quite comfortable. Finally, as at this point The Blight was forty-one, and certainly at this age deserved to be wedded, they offered to him a beautiful wife; the daughter of a highly respected man, who had then become a close friend of The Blight. He, without a moment's hesitation, accepted the offer. On his wedding day, the most beautiful and healthy of flowers grew in every inch of the town and the sun was bright and welcoming and the air never more comforting and clean. This he predicted and made certain its truth.

Indeed, The Blight was happy, and the days were sunny and bright. In fact, they were always sunny, crisp and bright. He tried to stir things up and predict otherwise. He would return home and at the moments without his wife around, he would attempt to draw out all of the old depressing memories, but found that he could not, as he truly and deeply loved the town.

You may not think this possible, but understand that the town had shown such an unpredictable change of face in response to his ability that The Blight could not find any other emotion than a warm and comfortable love.

He even tried to convince himself of the irrefutable truth that the town of Showver only bestowed such love and affection upon him because of his remarkable ability, but this was no use; this actually didn't concern him, because love, as it would seem, any love, was more than The Blight had ever received, and was perfect, regardless of its nature.

What could be wrong with bright, sunny and clear days? No rain, but the perfect amount of humidity remained for the crops and the town was never too dry. It was however, boring. Day after day, after day, nothing but the same exact temperature and same exact sun and same exact air and thus the same exact predictions.

Not long after the thought had crossed his mind, the towns-people started questioning The Blight. I should say he was now known as Edward Appleby, as his family name had been awarded to him.

They knew he could not change the weather, but they would become frustrated when his prediction implied more of the same old, same old. They wanted rain or at least a few more clouds in the sky. He wanted to give it to them, but he also wanted to stay in this warm and comfortable state. Happiness came about with the town's love, but now it seemed he would have to sacrifice this happiness simply to maintain such love.

Edward started to worry and to become frustrated with the entire predicament. His frustration wasn't steep, but it increased the heat outside. He predicted this may steadily increase and though they demanded predictions, they actually wanted change. Edward gave them change, but the only change he could provide was more heated or dry weather in response to his frustration. In fact, each person seemed to have a different idea as to how the weather should be and each time they received a prediction they became upset because it wasn't quite enough. Still Edward kept after the town with his kindly requested, but stern demands. After all, he could only predict the weather, but why would the town need predictions if it meant only hot days or the standard clear, sunny day.

Edward had become completely frustrated because his wife, as well as the rest of the town soon returned to their old ways and Edward quickly became Blight, not even *The* Blight. No longer would there be bright and sunny days. No longer would there be rain or variances. He had kept a steady, solid emotional state of hate and frustration, and with each passing day it grew more. Nobody cared to hear his predictions and he couldn't care to share them.

Blight awoke one morning to find his wife had left him and most of his belongings were gone. He proceeded outside in the old tattered clothes he had always worn when he was Blight. Outside, he saw the townspeople in their routines and he knew that soon enough, he would take to his. He predicted miserably, that things would go back to the way they were, which could have meant rain, but he made no such predictions as he would simply wore out his welcome as a weatherman. He wanted to find his wife before he allowed himself to fall back into place; he wanted to speak with her one last time.

Eventually, after several hours of wandering around, surrounded by stares, shaking heads and whispered words of disapproval, he had finally found her, the former Mrs. Appleby. She was, of course, with another man. I may have failed to mention that this particular woman was never so beautiful that she did not constantly need to have her beauty reaffirmed in the company of men who adored her.

Rage.

Everything that he believed he would soon just ignore and slip down somewhere inside himself and replace with a constant sorrow had become far too powerful to be controlled or stunted. He raced to her with a burning face and with every step, the ground rattled and the temperature outside grew by several degrees. The earth grunted fiercely as it burned and scorched through its once green face.

Once he had found himself before her, he saw that she was sweaty and pink, as were all, but Blight was nothing short of beaming bright red. He opened his mouth and everything in screeches and cries came billowing out. Each word he pummeled into her face, he became more and more infuriated, and with the final word finished, he truly exploded, turned his face to the burning sky and wailed. The once quaking ground exploded in turn and the entire town of Showver formed a great peaked magnanimous explosion; everything, especially Blight, for underneath his very feet the instantly formed volcano of mass destruction had sparked, was utterly obliterated and merged with the flaming mass of heated earth as ash. As quickly as everything stirred into chaos, it stilled and formed a large, cooled and solid mountain, which stood barren where once a town had been.

Blight, *The* Blight had one fault, and it existed in direct parallel to the fault within the town.

> *The mewing once more.*
> *I must take my leave.*
> *Thank you.*

SYMPATHY FOR THE LEVEE MAN

Every day I pass the levee.
And with it I pass its sole laborer,
A solitary man,
Who, day after day, fills the cracks,
And patches the holes.

Yet daily it rains and new ones form,
Disregarding his efforts.
The levee greets him at every meeting,
In this state of disrepair.

Though, at first I thought him a fool,
And meant to criticize his futile labor,
Instead, I offer a hand when it is free.

Knowing that I too toil over such cracks and holes,
Spending each day with trough and trowel.
My endeavor to lead a life devoted to,
And temporarily keep,
What can never be fixed.

And I wake with his thoughts,
And watch the downpour with his worry.
And am made weary knowing just as he,
That the levee will break.

That this solitary man,
Who alone has efforts spent,
Will be the first and likely the only,

To drown when it floods.

A DEPICTION OF WORDS UN-SPOKEN

Martin. In the greater part of his life, he may have only been so easily defined with a single, simple word. It would be this name. To most everyone, little more could really be said about him; little more was known, or likely, impossible to know.

From youth into adulthood, his story might've been described, by so many others, as diminutive; the unrequited life of the observer. Maybe once or twice, in all of his years, in those brief moments when he'd manage to free a thought to consider his existence, he likely would've agreed.

At birth, being the youngest, he'd already been given three siblings by his parents, Arthur and Lucy; these being his sister Sarah, and two brothers, Eric and Walter. He was welcomed and unwelcomed into the world simultaneously. He was loved by his parents, but the love seemed, like so many things in his life, to be a hand-me-down. He existed in the residuals of those who came before him.

To be sure, he was never resentful of his family. In a strange way, this second-hand nature suited him, as it was inconceivably difficult for him to express himself in personally distinct ways. On most occasions he could only muster what was often mistakenly perceived as a general apathy. With Martin, social interactions, communication, and, indeed expression at its most base, or creative forms were mostly lost concepts. It was only after thorough and exhaustive efforts on the behalf of Sarah, Arthur and Lucy that he was even able to speak at all. Thus, he was never quite sure of himself, or the world around him, and found it easier to live life without giving such things too much consideration, nor, at any given time, could he.

Quite capable of reading, memorizing, and calculating, Martin adhered to a very strict logic and often employed mimicry and recitation when independent, personal reactions were required. Often, he found himself following his siblings, both directly and indirectly; none more so than Sarah, who was closest in age. As a child, Sarah found that it was much to her own chagrin that he was always closest to her; after all, he wasn't the sister she'd wanted. As they grew older though, she'd eventually learned to tolerate the idea, and accepted that, if not always at a reasonable distance, Martin would be her shadow.

Sarah would even find herself on too many occasions, defending Martin, who was not only lax in the most inopportune moments, but almost always clumsily oblivious to the nature of his surroundings. Fights with boys were an inevitable part of Sarah's childhood. Other children, who typically garnered more independent and rambunctious demeanors, were not immediately accepting of the often intolerably passive Martin. Of these, Eric and Walter would most frequently face Sarah's sisterly, or perhaps motherly, wrath.

Countless efforts were made by both Martin's parents and his older sister to enkindle a sense of self, an independent identity within the boy, but it seemed impossible. Nothing ever took, and Sarah would find herself at odds with Arthur and Lucy, whom she believed had given up the task of building Martin. In truth, they hadn't. His parents had simply come to accept Martin as he was; a task that would prove a constant difficulty throughout Sarah's life.

After all, Martin wasn't inept. He could perform most tasks once demonstrated, and in fact, remembered nearly any piece of information he'd obtained with remarkable accuracy. He simply lacked the typically inherent ability to commit these tasks without direct outside influence. Lucy might have compared him to a leaf of some perfect geometric shape found drifting in the wind.

Saying he was brilliant in his own right, but far too reliant on the momentum provided by others, drifting without a semblance of passion or even the affectation to allude to such a thing. Arthur might have called him mindless and robotic.

To Sarah, it was if Martin was born incomplete. An identity, a personality, the essence of the individual are initialized at birth, perceived through expression and interaction, and are forged and tempered in the smoldering process of time. This didn't seem to happen with Martin. His thoughts, of which Sarah was certain the existence, were entirely his own and were never shared. Born the human embodiment of the blank slate, he remained, ever unchanging and lived with a steady dependence upon others, soaking up everything, but never directly interpreting or contributing. Sarah couldn't understand Martin, and refused to understand her parents. To plant a seed and watch it grow, only to have it never bear fruit, should be heartbreaking, and for Sarah, it was.

On the eve of a spring solstice, a ten year-old Martin followed a twelve year-old Sarah into the Bitterroot Forest as she ran from home. It was nearly midnight when Sarah snuck out of her room proceeding into the kitchen to make sandwiches, stealing fruit and water for her perceived long journey across the Canadian border. Martin, a notoriously light sleeper, shared a room with a fourteen year-old Walter, who could likely sleep through the Apocalypse. Martin, stirred by Sarah's late night excursion preparations, found his sister downstairs hurriedly stuffing her school backpack. Once he'd been made privy to the plan and given clear, succinct directions, as Martin always required, he retrieved a tent, two sleeping bags, a flashlight and a heater that was kept in the wood shed behind the house. Late that night, Martin and Sarah returned to sleep in a tent pitched quickly in a small clearing tucked between several large Ponderosa pines, watching over the moonlit night.

That following morning Sarah spent furiously explaining the need for their departure from home with Martin quietly listening, but not quite understanding.

"They don't get it. They never do anything. You know they were supposed to go to the school and meet with your teacher? Now I have Mrs. Tripp asking me every day, *'When am I going to see your parents?'* And she talks about you like you're re—she's just a fat, stupid cow."

"But why don't they talk to her? Am I supposed to take care of it? She wants to hold you back again. It's bullshit. And they can do something about it, but they won't."

"Don't you want to get out of that class?"

Sarah faced Martin and he watched as her face beamed red awaiting an answer.

"I...don't know. Patrick's gone."

"The mouse? Damn it Martin! Is that all you care about? You're too smart to be in that stupid class!"

Sarah turned away and shook her head in frustration.

"Mom says, *'He's just shy. He'll grow out of it, and in the meantime, he has you to watch after him.'* What the hell does that mean? I'm not always going to be there. You know that, right?"

Sarah returned her gaze to Martin and watched hoping the vacant look would leave his face. It didn't.

"You shouldn't have come with me. You should've just stayed home."

After a brief moment of silence exchanged between the siblings Martin replied;

"I...I always go with you."

"But that's just it, Martin. You can't always follow me everywhere I go. You need to learn to do things on your own. Don't you want to?"

Martin could only respond to Sarah's quizzical and demanding look with confusion and fear as his previously unassuming visage began to contort and tears welled up in his eyes. It was something he'd thought about often, but it seemed too great a struggle to overcome, and so he'd forced himself to ignore such aspirations, especially if they could only be achieved without Sarah.

"I always go with you."

Sarah could feel the instant, sharp grasp of sympathy and guilt as she watched her brother lightly tremor with worry. It was only Sarah who would see these slight emotional responses, and they'd only ever come when she was angry with him. She reached into her bag, retrieved an old friendship bracelet with worn-to-brown edges, wrapped it around Martin's wrist and hugged him briefly.

"I know you do, Martin...I know."

Martin watched his own hand as he slowly twisted the bracelet around his wrist back and forth. He silently counted with repeated rhythms. Through his mind raced countless subjects as he desperately tried to assimilate coherence in the chaos. He wanted to say something to Sarah, something meaningful, or at least, show her how much he was trying. As always, his mind repeatedly stabbed at itself like flailing skewers struggling to pin down any portion of the swirling mass of collected information that would not stay still for even a single moment. He could do nothing. Instead, he kept with the task at hand, turning the bracelet around his wrist, as it was the only thing his mind allowed, and with this entrancing motion, Martin was able to find peace as his mind acquired a sense of order through focus and isolation. He'd often found a comfort in this serenity of ignorance, as all thought seemed to become absent, or at least, quiet momentarily with the simple repetition. It was as if it all worked in polarizing opposites, either all thoughts colliding and ricocheting through his chaotic mind or nothing, save a single almost obsessively focused and strangely galvanizing reprise of constants.

Sarah watched as her brother fixated and despaired. She didn't see the appeasement attained through repetitive calculation. Instead, she had only seen obsessive, mindless behavior, and as always, it worried her, deeply.

"Come on, Martin. Let's get all of this packed up. We've got a lot of ground to cover. First, we're going to see if we can hitch a ride to Missoula and get out of this backwards place."

Martin looked up at Sarah, donning his blank expression once more. It only served to frustrate her as she knew anyone else would question her reasoning, but Martin would always follow without hesitation.

"It's not a good idea, is it? I don't know what the hell we'd even do. I just...I can't go back there...At least, not yet."

"So what'll we do, Martin? You decide."

Martin stared for a moment as his eyes twitched lightly from side to side in rapid movements. He then jerked his head down and stared once more into his hand rotating the bracelet as he counted every stitch.

"Martin..." Sarah sighed and stood to survey her surroundings.

"Well, we're not going home. Maybe we'll just camp out here for a while. Mom and Dad can sweat a little. Absence makes the heart grow fonder, right?"

Martin had finished counting the knots, threads, and every possible color combination to be made with the multi-colored bracelet and had moved on to mentally unraveling the entire construct to determine the length of each thread involved.

"Hey, let's go hiking! Dad never took you to Lolo Peak, did he?"

The first quarter mile of the hike was very steep and thus the two kept a modest pace. They'd brought with them a couple of water bottles, one of which Martin specifically insisted he carry... without so many words. A water bottle, not quite filled to the lid, as were the others, with no indication of the amount of fluid held within, served as another perplexity with several solutions awaiting discovery through logical progression. As they walked, he tilted the bottle back and forth watching the cascading rhythm of the water flow along the curvature of the bottle's supposed ergonomic design.

Sarah watched her brother closely as it was clear he was paying very little attention to his steps. After his third misstep, Sarah yanked the bottle from his hand with great aggravation. She'd expected resistance and based on her estimate had applied a particularly exaggerated amount of force when ripping the bottle from Martin's grasp. Martin, however, was only gingerly holding the water in order to minimize the effect of his grip upon the water's displacement. Being incorrect in her assumption, Sarah threw herself backwards. Though she'd only shifted her stance slightly, it was just enough to lose footing. Slipping, Sarah tumbled and, though clasping hurriedly and making several attempts to brace herself, fell beyond the edge of trail.

Martin leapt towards her, but fell short. Laying on the edge of the trail, he could only stare down as Sarah plummeted, screaming as she fell several dozen feet. Attempting to yell after her, Martin couldn't find his voice and instead raced down the cliff as quickly as he could. He'd found her unconscious, but breathing. Nudging Sarah several times, Martin cried in disbelief as she failed to respond. Panicked, he still couldn't find the ability to speak, even just to say her name. Several moments passed as he struggled with decisions, before finally lifting her body to his chest. He trekked back up the cliff angling his footing to ensure any fall could only injure him, but leave her unscathed.

Martin's mind lost all focus and all movement was delegated to his subconscious. His body was given the simple order to carry Sarah and continue walking as far as his legs were physically capable. This was all he could do, and he'd hoped desperately, it was all that would be needed.

With eyes blurred by tears, Martin raced past the tent where they'd slept and hurried blindly through the forest. In any case, with his mind so thoroughly obscured by a cloud of thought, sight would've been of no regard.

Adrenaline carried Martin as he carried Sarah, and nothing else was of any use.

Leaving town, in search for their two missing children, Arthur and Lucy sped along the highway looking for forest road exits. As Lucy combed the east side of the road looking for any immediate pull-outs or indications of recent activity, she hoped that her daughter would not have strayed too far from the highway. In the distance, quickly walking along the highway, Lucy spotted a figure, and as they quickly approached, she made certain the identification.

Martin's senses were largely impaired in his state of panic, so he simply did not hear as his parents shouted after him. He continued as quickly as he could, not certain of his directions, his sister's sustained injuries, or his ability to continue much further. All of this and none of this occurred nearly simultaneously as his mind became occupied with hundreds of current, past and future scenarios.

Still Martin wept, and this continued as his parents retrieved him and his sister. He couldn't answer the questions they excitedly bellowed, and he could do nothing to ease the fear and pain he shared with them as they quickly placed Sarah's body in the car. Instead, he stood motionless and blankly stared through the blurred, traipsing fluid which coated his eyes.

Arthur made attempts to help Martin into the vehicle, and with a strong grasp even tried to forcefully pull him. He did his best not to display his panicked frustration with Martin, but the facade was becoming difficult to maintain.

"Get in the car Martin! NOW!"

Arthur nearly wrestled his son's stubborn body into submission before Lucy interjected;

"Please Martin, Sarah needs you with her."

And, if only momentarily, Martin was able to regain control and move his body to comply.

After surgery, Sarah remained in the hospital for four days followed by three weeks spent at home recovering from a broken wrist, leg and rib. During this time, Martin refused to leave her side and in solemn silence he guarded over her.

Martin refused to speak even a single word throughout the entire ordeal, and though he was often prone to silence, a response of any kind from him, then appeared entirely nonexistent. Even Sarah could not coax Martin to reply, though she made multiple laborious attempts.

Retreating into his mind, Martin struggled to find comfort in the familiar, if not perplexing world, of his thoughts. The reality before him was too difficult. He'd wished he could have somehow have stopped Sarah and rather than following as he could only ever seem to do, he could have voiced his opinion and persuaded her to return home. These thoughts were pointless, and this Martin knew, but still, as with most thoughts he'd formed, they remained and pursued him relentlessly.

At the end of the third week Sarah returned to school, as did Martin, but things were different and though Sarah was still recovering she'd found herself more concerned for her brother than ever before. He would not speak. He would not react in any way to anything said to him. As Sarah stepped out of the school bus to rush to meet her friends, she turned back to see Martin standing beneath a tree facing it and staring with little movement.

"Come on Martin, I'm the one who got hurt not you. Let's get you to class!"

As Sarah grasped Martin's arm to pull him away from the tree, he not only resisted, but grabbed her hand, squeezed it and jerked his arm back and otherwise, stubbornly remained unmoving.

"Forget it Martin! I've spent almost a month dealing with this. I don't know what to say to you anymore."

Sarah huffed and sped away and just before reuniting with the small group of girls giggling and recounting the previous day's events, she turned back once more to check on Martin.

Slowly, Martin backed away from the tree, and staring down to his feet, he lumbered off in the direction of his classroom, looking as if he was committing no thought to any action, relying wholly upon repetitive, subconscious movement.

Sarah shook her head, "Martin…"

She returned to her friends just as they began to make their way to class.

During class, Sarah could hardly focus, her thoughts thoroughly fixed upon her brother whom she feared was losing whatever
battle he'd constantly encountered within his mind. In an attempt
to alleviate some of her worry, Sarah began listing symptoms she
noticed in her brother. Every indicative action, inaction and routine she could remember him ever performing. These she listed in
chronological order, sectioned into measures of severity, his recent
state being his most severe.

What use this information would be, Sarah didn't know. She
could attempt to bring it to the attention of the school counselor,
but it would likely be of little use, after all, the majority of the listed
items were entirely categorical for Martin and everyone was well
aware of what they seemed resigned to consider traits.

The bell rang declaring the lunch hour.

Quickly, Sarah finished the very last item on her list; the in-
cident that morning and Martin's abnormally violent refusal to
comply.

Martin nearly always joined Sarah with her friends during
lunch. Her friends tolerated the unwanted presence, but preferred
Sarah's strange brother be kept at a distance. Indeed, it was only
after their first attempt to bar Martin from their group that they'd
learned Sarah's remarkable capacity for rage. They might have ban-
ished her as well, but Sarah was popular with the boys, and though
she found no immediate use of this, her friends seemed to enjoy
the frequent flirtatious visits Sarah would often draw.

Martin did not join Sarah and her friends. Instead, after some
searching, Sarah found him sitting under the same tree he'd affixed himself to that morning. He sat motionless and alone, gently
touching the grass and staring at his hands. He was clearly lost, and
for a moment Sarah felt a sincere dread in that she may never again
be able to get through to her brother. She swallowed several times
with painful force as she tried to keep herself from tearing up.

She approached Martin slowly and leaned down as she moved
in closer.

"I'm sorry about what I said earlier Martin. Why don't you come hang out with me and the girls?"

No response. He moved, but only his hands, following the same dazed sways as they gently brushed the tips of the grassy blades.

"Martin...Please..."

Moving his head slightly, Martin tensed his neck muscles and clenched his jaws. He still didn't look up, and Sarah watched as he tremored lightly with great effort applied in his refusal to acknowledge her.

Sarah began to cry and left her brother beneath the tree. She didn't return to her friends; she couldn't face them and they certainly wouldn't understand. Instead, she hurried to the library.

Martin, too, could feel the tears as they slowly created paths down the sides of his face. At that moment, he hated everything, but most of all, he hated himself. He panicked silently for the entire lunch hour. Wondering among countless other thoughts, if he'd destroyed a relationship he'd struggled desperately his entire life to maintain with the one person who'd shown him the most compassion.

The only allies Martin ever had in his life he'd inherited, and those few he could count on one hand. Had he his own way, he'd have no enemies and would be able to converse freely with whomever he pleased, but it simply wasn't so. He could not afford to lose his sister. With most, this thought might be enough to propel the bearer into action, but with Martin it simply repeated itself over and over again not allowing him to address it, but forcing him into further panic.

So until the bell rang finally giving Martin some way to logically break his own infinite loop, he spiraled uncontrollably.

Sarah, however, spent the remainder of the lunch period in the library. She combed over her list and perused through the only book she could find in the school library related to psychology.

Can a broken mind be fixed?

Sarah inquired and found that though the two-thousand page book may have an answer, it would require more than one lunch period to find it.

Martin's buried somewhere inside himself. There's got to be a way to bring him out. What will he become if I can't help him?

"Sarah!"

"What?" Sarah turned and looked up to find her mother staring down over her as she sat in the living room recliner reading the newly acquired psychology book.

"Is Martin okay?" Lucy gestured to Martin, sitting at the kitchen table staring at another water bottle his mother had given him.

"Am I my brother's keeper?" Sarah made no attempt to soften the snide remark.

"Sarah! Go sit with Martin."

Sarah complied, but she knew it would make no difference; "It's not gonna matter."

Lucy shook her head and returned to the kitchen to begin baking the lasagna she'd prepared for dinner.

At dinner, both Sarah and Lucy worriedly checked Martin and his plate in brief intervals as they lightly picked at their own servings. Martin sat as he had since returning home from school, slowly turning the water bottle and staring into the distorted reflections in the water. Fifteen minutes passed in this manner before Arthur interjected;

"Would someone please take that damned water bottle from him?"

"Arthur! Leave him alone." Lucy sternly protested her husband's request, but, as was often the case, it had little impact.

"No. He needs to eat. Martin! Eat your dinner."

Though this could have escalated with Martin ultimately oblivious to anything to be found outside of the water bottle, his entranced state was interrupted as Sarah withdrew the bottle from his grasp. She did so gently this time, and he provided no resistance.

For a moment, Martin stared into his plate with no reaction. Everyone except Eric and Walter watched and waited. Martin began to eat. Of the grand list of the activities in which Martin found difficulty, eating was not one of them. One of the only human acts with which Martin had no issue, he actually enjoyed eating and nothing more so than his mother's lasagna.

Two months passed in mostly the same manner. Martin committed to his new mindless routine spent alone for a brief couple of weeks, but eventually resumed his previous habit of following Sarah with a similar lack of consciousness.

Sarah, however, did not return to her group of friends. With Martin by her side, she continued spending her free moments at school in the library and at home fully dedicated to her psychological studies. She'd expanded her research to include several encyclopedias and three additional psychology books she'd acquired temporarily from the public library.

Though Sarah hadn't completely dissolved her interactions with her brother, they'd become far more limited as she delved deeply into the studies that one day may help him.

Because Martin didn't necessarily require interaction, he found their new tradition acceptable, and as long as he could remain in Sarah's presence, he rarely felt the need to panic. But even so, he'd remained completely disinclined socially and had yet to speak a single word since the day of Sarah's fall.

Sarah's intentions were innocent and pure, but as she continued to read and began to understand the difficulties Martin faced on a constant basis, she started to realize how her own intentions were misguided. She thought of Martin as broken, and though it was out of love and compassion that she sought to fix him, but it was coupled with her own desire to pursue a life not so significantly intertwined with the life of her brother.

In these two months, she'd learned that though Martin was born with the mind of disorder, helping him in such a way that he would never need her again would be impossible. Instead, she decided she would commit her life to helping Martin and others like him to lead a life as comfortably and as socially rich as could be managed.

"Martin. Martin, please look at me."

Martin, sitting just beside Sarah at the table in the farthest corner of the school library, struggled for a moment and turned to face his sister.

"Martin, I'm sorry, I always thought I could make you...more like me, or, more like the other kids at school. I thought you'd be better off if you could manage without help. And while I still think you need to try to be more independent in some ways, I was wrong and I promise you I will always be there to help you."

"You don't show it and you don't say it, but I know you're thinking...constantly, and deeply, more than any of us could ever hope to. And while that means things are racing through your mind that the world probably couldn't begin to comprehend, it also means you'll always have difficulty expressing even the simplest of thoughts. I hope someday that you'll find some way to show me or tell me what you're thinking..."

Martin heard his sister's words; through the haze of disarray they'd found their way in and he'd committed every word to memory. If the words similarly could find their way, he would've thanked his sister and assured her he would always try for her. While this sentiment was too difficult for him to verbalize, it was not lost as he simply replied for the first time in several months.

"Sarah."

And as she embraced her brother, she understood.

At age twenty-seven Sarah received her doctorate in Social and Behavioral Science and in two short years, she'd opened her own clinic in Prince George, British Columbia. She'd finally crossed the Canadian border as she always intended and with her, just as with her first attempt at age twelve, Martin followed.

Throughout the preceding years, Martin had advanced in small bounds and was able to socialize, even with strangers, briefly from time to time. Though this would always be in the form of short awkwardly spoken segments, it was a considerable improvement. It meant that Martin was starting to manage the chaotic environment of his mind, if only in some small way.

He continued with his obsessive behaviors, but it had become apparent to others, by way of Sarah, that Martin was gifted with an incredible mathematically inclined intellect and he, too, was able to pursue a more focused education which later resulted in a master's degree in mathematics.

With Sarah's assistance, Martin found employment designing software encryption for a computer-based telecommunication company and its subsidiaries; employing him utilizing such tele-communication, thus he was able to work in an office in the same building where Sarah operated her clinic.

Two years later, Sarah married a fellow psychologist by the name of Peter Haskell, and in short time they'd found a new home and began sharing the clinic. Martin was given residence in a small guest house located just behind the Haskell's residence. Nearly every night the three shared dinner together and Martin added Peter to the very short list of friends with whom he'd become comfortable.

"How do you like the rollatini, Martin? Sarah tells me you've never had it before. I'll let you in on a secret…I've never made it before. I hope it tastes alright."

Smiling, Peter addressed Martin and awaited his response. Martin, with a mouth full of ricotta and eggplant nodded, affirming his approval.

Peter laughingly replied; "Good!"

"You're a wonderful cook, Peter. It's just too bad you wasted all of that time becoming a third-rate psychologist." Sarah prodded her husband with banter.

Suddenly, a great raucous laughter escaped Martin's mouth finding both Sarah and Peter in a short state of shock. Never in the year had he come to know Martin had Peter ever heard him laugh; and never in Sarah's entire life had she even considered Martin capable of such.

The husband and wife broke their startled silence and joined Martin in laughter.

The following morning, Peter, Sarah and Martin arrived at the clinic to find a young woman waiting outside of the entrance clutching a stack of papers to her chest. She appeared frantic and immediately Sarah readied her first line of evocative questions.

But after asking her first question, Sarah quickly learned this wasn't needed.

"Hello. How may I help you?"

"I'm sorry I must appear a mess. I've been all over this city applying and I was told to always apply in person as soon as the clinics open to make a good first impression. I woke up late and rushed over here…I…I guess shouldn't even be saying this…Can I start again?"

The young woman made no apparent effort to conceal her frayed nerves and nearly dropped her papers as she erratically threw out gestures accompanying her words.

"Please let me help you."

Sarah retrieved the papers from the young woman as Peter unlocked the clinic entrance.

"And please…you can relax, we're pretty informal here. Why don't you step inside?"

Sarah stepped aside and waited as the young woman walked into the building. She turned to see her brother standing motionless in the parking lot watching the woman as she entered the clinic and staring with an expression Sarah had never seen Martin bear.

Martin's mind was clear. The typically tumultuous and misdirecting ruminations that would prevent any number of physical interactions were missing and his mind yielded only one concern. He thought only of the strange, new woman, and he was infatuated.

Alice, she revealed to be her name, when attempting to apply for a job that was not actually available. She'd calmed her initial jitters and explained that she'd recently received her bachelor's degree in psychology and had been trying for some time to find a clinic that would offer her an internship.

She appeared qualified, and Peter seemed to think she would be an asset as it would relieve him of some of the unwanted duties Sarah had delegated to him. Sarah remained unsure and as she accepted Alice's documents, she informed her that she would contact her shortly with her decision.

After the three returned home, Sarah opened a discussion over dinner with regards to Alice.

"I think she's qualified enough. And you can't deny that we need the help. I looked over our finances earlier today and it is feasible."

"You just don't want to be the clinic's receptionist anymore."

Sarah smiled at her husband and looked to Martin, who stared at her expectantly as if he was sitting on the verge of a great speech, which should compel her to hire the young woman immediately. Instead he mumbled, paused and introduced a statement of which he was very certain.

"I...I like her."

A quizzical look was caught momentarily between Sarah and Peter as they attempted to understand what was occurring and how they should feel about it.

Alice was five years Martin's junior, and though apparently prone to nervousness, she appeared socially functional. Sarah could think of too many scenarios in which Martin's infatuation with the woman could be disastrous as it presented social difficulties he'd never experienced and may, likely, be unable to manage. His directness and certainty was welcomed, he was voicing an opinion, and Sarah had never known Martin to do such a thing.

Martin and Alice would both find themselves in a safe environment in the clinic and Sarah, Peter and Alice were educated thoroughly in emotional behavior. It was reasonable to think it could work and they would assist Martin should he experience any emotional difficulties. Peter was certainly accurate in that they needed the help. Beyond all of this, and though she was simultaneously worried, Sarah found herself delighted with what she saw as an opportunity to enkindle Martin's emotional and social progression.

Alice was hired, and Sarah thought it best, given that she would be working closely with her immediate family, that she be introduced to her brother, who'd hidden in his office during the interview.

"Alice, I would like you to meet my brother, Martin. He shares this building with us. He's a freelance cryptographer...and our un-official accountant."

As Sarah introduced him, Martin stood strangely erect in his stance, staring at the young woman with an expression she'd mis-took for disapproval. It was Martin's most common expression and behind it, he bore anything but disapproval.

"He-"

Alice was about to commit to the introductory ritual before,

"Martin! I...I'm..."

He began to struggle and could feel his face beam red as his jaws quivered. It seemed an eternity as he screamed in his mind and tried, dearly, to turn and escape to the security of his office. Alice, made completely aware of the situation as she watched Martin nearly quaking in introverted anguish, applied her most sincere and calming tones as she addressed him.

"I'm Alice. It's great to meet you Martin. Your sister speaks very highly of you."

In truth, Alice knew no more about Martin than she'd learned with Sarah's introduction, but it was a safe assumption. The red blanketing Martin's face retreated quickly and he bowed nervously before making his retreat.

"I hope I didn't scare him off."

"Oh, no. Of course not. Martin's very shy, but I'm sure he'll warm up to you. He didn't say a word to Peter when they first met."

Peter, within earshot of his wife, could certainly attest to this. In fact, in all of time he'd known Martin, he'd heard him speak a total of five words. In this sense, Alice had already made far more progress with Martin than had he.

Even so, three days passed with Martin saying not one word to Alice; even when confronted. When greeted, he merely responded with a wave or a nod depending on the context.

But on the third day, Martin surprised his sister once more. As Alice sat at the receptionist's desk searching through papers for a specific patient's form, she was approached by her employer's brother.

"Hello, Alice."

With these two words, now floating in the silent air, Martin stood staring at the desk's surface nervously awaiting a reply while fighting the intolerable need to panic.

Initially taken aback, Alice too was silent, but knew she'd just received a social queue from one of the most unlikely of people and if she didn't respond, the tense silence bearing down upon Martin would not simply give way. Though she'd been given only brief moments with Martin, she somehow felt she knew him personally. In truth, she'd been hoping he would make such efforts.

"How are you today, Martin?"

Alice expected no reply, but hoped at least, her cordiality would put him at ease.

Far more than she could have expected, it did.

In Martin's mind, a strange new clarity burgeoned as it seemed the hazes of bedlam began to dissipate, and though it was a slow process, he was immediately able to identify the source of its influx.

It was Alice's voice.

"I'm...good. You?"

He replied with the last two words being spurted out nearly simultaneously in the form of a single word. The kink initiated his internal reproach.

Again, his mind was soothed with an amicable reply,

"I'm doing very well. Slowly, but surely, I'm learning the ropes around here and Sarah and Peter are both so wonderful!"

Sarah, at a distance, listened to the conversation and couldn't quite think of what to make of it. It was clear that Martin had strong feelings for Alice, but his interaction with her was nothing short of astonishing.

Out of her seat, Sarah watched her brother through the doorway of her office and could not help but beam at the sight. Her brother's moods were never entirely apparent on the surface, but at that moment, looking at him, she was certain. He was content.

Martin, in response to Alice's friendly assurance, smiled as well. Within his mind, he'd found a simple tranquility, if only momentarily, and thus the resulting smile was his most honest.

The remainder of the day continued in its standard proceedings as did the following few with Martin making short and sporadic visits to the receptionist's desk, each time obliging slightly greater efforts to converse.

After two weeks had passed in such steady progression, at the invite of Sarah, Alice joined the small family for dinner.

It was a pleasant night and Alice, with the benevolent demeanor the others had come to recognize in her, found herself in well accommodating company. Stories were shared as were laughs which found even Martin participating.

Finally by the end of the night as goodbyes were being said, Martin offered more words than he ever had before. As Alice approached the door with intent to leave, Martin stopped her.

"Alice…"

"I…I'm glad you're working at the clinic."

While these words were not necessarily profound, the context behind them, most certainly carried great weight. As Martin smiled, as he'd recently become accustomed, Alice leaned in and kissed his cheek.

Sarah, in a jovial mood until this encounter, found the act troubling. *What is she thinking?*

She'd quickly envisioned a horrible scenario. Martin who'd she considered by no means emotionally mature would expect far too much of this otherwise inconsequential act, and should he be met with an unfavorable reality, no matter how gently offered by a sweet girl. Sarah had only once felt the violent side of her brother and while it was instantaneous and minor, Sarah feared any reaction to a situation neither she nor Martin had ever encountered.

And it's all my doing.

Sarah turned to Peter with concern, deeply engraved as lines above her brow.

"What was I thinking?"

Embracing his wife Peter laughed.

"I think you worry too much. Martin may be more capable than you realize."

Planting a kiss just beside Sarah's ear, Peter whispers,

"What a great mother our children will find in you."

"Peter…Martin, he…he's changed."

Martin still standing at the closed door with his face refusing to release the blood flushed in his cheeks, considers the implications of the kiss, and is hopeful but finds himself to be troubled as well. Hundreds of potential scenarios, both positive and negative collide and react in his mind. He considers that even with his most wishful thoughts, Alice may require more from him than he could ever hope to provide. It was true that he was gaining a composure he'd never experienced, but how permanent could that be?

He'd meant to tell Sarah any number of things throughout his life. He'd meant to prevent her fall and ease her mind in regards to their parents and the school. He'd meant to have friends and socialize and make insightful observations when called upon to do so, but he couldn't.

And Alice. He would tell her he loves her, and that he'd always questioned the significance of a life so thoroughly dependent upon that of others. How, when seeing her for the first time, he'd lost that question entirely and replaced it with the firm belief that his very existence prior was strictly transitive to that moment. His mind left certain that a world without Alice would find him unnecessary.

But after a week's worth of considerable preparation, he'd only been able to tell her he was glad, and frankly, those words found even him surprised.

While he'd felt the incredible rush of elation and a perfect sense that all at once everything was simply as it should be, he'd followed this with dread and an insurmountable fear that the future before him would be one which finds him thoroughly incapable.

The next morning found both Martin and Sarah in varying levels of disconcertion, with Martin experiencing the more severe. In fact, without words, he'd refused to join Peter and Sarah at the office and insisted that he remain home, by way of hiding in his room and refusing to unlock his door.

Sarah wasn't concerned. Instead she found herself somewhat relieved. She'd expected an enamored Martin to be racing to the door like a love-sick puppy. Though she correctly assumed his reason for staying, she thought it best to allow Martin the time he'd require to process the night's events. She was only reluctant in leaving him home alone.

So Peter accepted an offer he hesitantly presented. He stayed home to watch after Martin; a task he neither dreaded nor considered with any particular enthusiasm. Peter had only ever experienced Martin with the preferred buffer provided by his wife.

At the clinic, Sarah met Alice and quickly prepared a lecture, but she was refused the opportunity.

"Good morning, Doctor Haskell. Where are Martin and Peter?"

Alice's concern for Martin's absence was genuine and apparent to Sarah. Her concern for Peter was simply tacked on. It was very likely she assumed that Peter was watching after Martin.

"Good morning, Alice. I'm afraid Martin isn't feeling well and Peter stayed home to watch after him."

"I'm sorry to hear that. I hope it's nothing serious. Poor Martin...I...That actually brings me to something I need to speak with you about."

Again the concern was gleamed in Alice's soft eyes as she looked to Sarah with a greater apprehension than she'd presented when first they'd met. Her words found no ease in their presentation.

"I was thinking about last night...about Martin, specifically. I love working with you three...I'd hoped to intern at a clinic... really just to learn the ropes, as they say. I never expected I'd be blessed to work with such wonderful people. And Martin...at first, I was certain I'd never hear him speak. And somehow, that thought really bothered me. It wasn't that I was worried that it would make things uncomfortable for me..."

Sarah followed Alice and directed her to sit in a waiting room chair. She was beginning to tear up and Sarah could feel herself fighting the urge to do the same. She knew the words that would follow and awaited them with severe anticipation.

"I thought, how terrible for him. I look into his eyes and I see millions of thoughts waiting behind them. I see the words trapped somewhere...and I thought, how horrible that I could never hope to bring a single one out. And somehow, I desperately wanted to..."

Sarah could feel her throat tensing as she swallowed in hopes to prevent the inevitable, but as Alice repeated every thought Sarah herself had once encountered in regards to Martin, she couldn't refrain and she too slowly shed tears.

"So when Martin spoke to me the first time...My heart jumped, and I was so excited. To think of the amount of effort it required... maybe it's conceit, but I felt like...maybe it meant something...and I know Martin is...I know he has trouble with these things. And I would never want to make things any more difficult for him than they already are...But I'm certain, I've been certain..."

Sarah began to weep openly. She had heard in Alice's voice, words she'd never once considered another would speak in regards to her brother. Since childhood, she had fought with her parents and she had fought with her teachers. She had constantly fought with herself and made every attempt to convince everyone that she had no desire to watch after her brother, but in Martin she had discovered purpose. It was her compassion that ensured Martin was never left wanting anything, least of all, love, and it was as if to a mother Alice was confessing her love for her son.

Through tears Sarah gave her blessing and made great attempts to regain composure. She'd hoped Martin would find himself capable of requital, but her stomach churned with the worry of possible outcomes. The day's procession was filled with awkward silence as the two women struggled to occupy themselves completely with their work.

Peter found a far less harrowing experience as he attempted to console Martin.

The first three hours were spent with Martin in silence on the other side of his locked door and Peter periodically knocking and politely requesting to enter. Eventually Martin conceded and opened his door. The silence ensued as Martin refused to speak, but Peter was glad to find that, otherwise, he seemed alright.

Indeed, Martin was. Or, at least, he was feeling quite the same as he'd had the few days before. In his mind he had twisted and struggled through the varying depictions of future scenarios, grasping at them as they swam by in cerebral currents. But one repeated and insisted its presence be dominant. It remained by his favor and it became his goal.

Martin didn't want to avoid Alice. He wanted, desperately, to confess his every thought to her. But with that likely out of the question, he would instead be in her presence, as often as he could and as often as she would allow. He didn't know how she felt, and he struggled with the attempt to fathom her feelings. Simply, he figured, if she didn't want him around, she would need only let him know. And that would be the end of it. But, because he hated this thought, he had decided it wasn't possible, thus the trepidation subsided and he made every attempt to ensure that it remain at bay.

At dinner that night, Sarah, Peter and Martin said very little to one another, but the evening didn't proceed in total silence and before the night found its end, the disquiet filling the air was allowed to dissipate.

"Martin, do you plan to return to your office tomorrow? Peter says you seem to be feeling better."

In a confirming response, Martin simply nodded his head and continued to eat.

Sarah turned to Peter and offered a brief, weary smile. It was evident that her mind was occupied with something she wished to discuss, but if Peter had learned anything about his wife, it was that it was never wise to press her. He figured in time she'd reveal her thoughts. As he had become accustomed to her brother, who simply never shared his thoughts, he'd found great patience in this regard.

Before giving way to sleep, the couple discussed Martin and Alice; the events that had taken place, those to come, and, at length, Martin's potential behavioral changes. It was reasoned that to attempt to halt any interaction between the two would have far greater consequences than letting them proceed as they may. The hope too, was present; that such an unlikely circumstance could lead to a successful and meaningful relationship, one that would finally enable Martin to become Martin in the presence of others.

Martin and Peter joined the women at the clinic the following morning. The moment of Martin's encounter with Alice that day, left a significant mark on all witnessing parties.

Alice, who was in the parking lot, having just exited her vehicle, was greeted by the three. Peter and Sarah made way to the clinic entrance, but Martin approached Alice directly. For a moment, the two stood face to face, Martin staring down into Alice's youthful eyes. Martin then embraced her, and with no resistance, she eased into his welcomed grasp. Sarah stood watching as Peter held open the clinic door. Both were fixated on the strange, but tender sight.

Sarah laughed. She wasn't entirely certain why the scene before her warranted such a reaction, but she laughed just the same. In the time before, she'd thought about how she would be losing Martin and how her tireless efforts found such little progress yet Alice, in so many weeks had made Martin anew. The thought had depressed her, worried her, and left her envious, but now it simply struck her as humorous. It could only ever have worked in such a way, as so many things seem to; years of care and dedication and in mere moments the most significant changes are brought about by something so unexpected and seemingly unlikely.

Weeks passed with Martin's social behavior improving sporadically, but with both welcome and support from Sarah, Peter and especially, Alice. His participation in conversations increased greatly, and though he only ever had a few words to offer, he offered them nearly every time he was called upon to do so. Within the murky depths of contemplation, Martin was finding a new order and was given access to mental realms previously unavailable.

Frequently, Alice would visit, join the siblings for dinner and even share in their outings. In short time, she had become part of their small family. Sarah's fear of losing her brother seemed to fade as it became evident that Alice had no intentions of causing such separation.

On one occasion, the two couples ventured to a forested pasture where Peter recommended spending the day and having a picnic lunch. It was an hour's drive that passed quickly with the jovial telling of jokes, a few childhood stories and even brief exchanges of psychological insights, which Alice greatly enjoyed and Martin merely ignored in thoughtful silence. Martin understood and appreciated that he was sharing the vehicle with three psychologists, but in truth, he'd always been uncomfortable when in the presence of such discussions, as it caused him to become very self-aware. He believed that, at times, they could sense this, but they in the fervor of heated discussion, would often be made oblivious. So he had learned at such times, to retreat into his mind, where more recently, he'd found serenity.

"There are few things as pleasant as a picnic eaten in perfect comfort."

Peter decided to begin the affair with a quote from his favored author. Sarah had heard far too many of the words of Mr. Maugham from her husband and decided it best to cease what could become a series of such quotes.

"Don't start. And don't either of you let him quote novels to you. He won't stop once he's started."

Peter laughed and began another approach.

"How are you enjoying the scones, Alice?"

He directed his attention to the young woman, who was fever-ishly devouring the treat, and took a short sip of his Shiraz.

She giggled and responded.

"Oh, I must be making a pig of myself...but these are wonder-ful. Who made these?"

"That would the expert baker, Sarah. I've told her she makes the best scones of the great north. But, of course, she doesn't believe a word of it."

Sarah smiled as Peter gently squeezed her hand.

"Wonderful."

Martin's typical short verbal offering was greeted with quick, light laughs from the already giddy Alice.

"I think Alice is very much enjoying the Shiraz."

"Indeed I am..."

Alice continued to snicker as she responded to Sarah's quip.

"...And I'll add, the greatest company I ever could hope to keep."

Martin seemed to appreciate the sentiment and added,

"Cheers!"

Before the delightful excursion had ended, the two bottles of Shiraz neatly packed with fine intentions had been thoroughly en-joyed to completion.

After a couple of months, Sarah had become concerned with the new arrangement. She'd allowed herself some excitement in the idea that her brother would achieve some independence. While he was far more sociable than he'd ever been, she had worried that with the security afforded by familiarity, his improvement was inhibited. She had felt it was time he attempt to breach his comfort zone, with Alice's help.

"Alice, may I speak with you for a moment?"

Sarah directed Alice to her office and both took a seat.

"I can't tell you how much it means to me…what you've done for my brother…that you've come into his life. And at first…I, I wasn't fond of the idea. I just couldn't envision it in any positive light. But I was wrong. I guess I wasn't having enough faith in Martin…in you…"

She seemed to trail off for a moment as she directed her attention to the office window overlooking a small patch of grass with a single pine tree. A minute passed as Sarah second guessed herself. *Maybe it's best that things remain as they are. Would it be so upsetting to Martin that he leave his sister's side? He has Alice now. He has himself.*

"Sarah?" Alice expressed her momentary concern.

"I think you should take Martin…away for a few days. Just you and him. I think…I hope, he's ready for it and it would be good for him. It would be good for you both."

Looking to Alice, Sarah seemed to express regret in the suggestion.

"Is that all? Sarah, you had me worried. Of course! I've been thinking that myself. I just wasn't sure what could be considered premature. But I think you're right. I think he's ready and we'll have a splendid time. I already have a few ideas…"

Alice excitedly smiled to Sarah who immediately relieved her face of deep concern and returned the smile and, to a lesser degree, the enthusiasm.

"I'm sorry I was being so severe. I just wasn't sure myself. As Peter would say, *the oft predictable Martin can sometimes be very unpredictable.*"

The two shared a laugh and few additional words before Alice returned to her desk and Sarah to reviewing patient's records.

Alice joined Martin and his siblings for dinner once again and revealed her plans to an anticipating couple and an individual who was completely unaware.

To the other's relief, Martin seemed to greatly favor the idea and lifted his glass to indicate his enthusiastic approval. The rest did the same as Peter proclaimed, "À la vôtre."

As the darkness of the night dampened the light and spirit born of the day, the three became fatigued and Alice took her leave.

Alice, still thoroughly excited, climbed into her car and exited the driveway into the typically absent street, unaware of the oncoming motorist. The oncoming driver, through the assistance of an intoxicated haze, was completely unaware of his surroundings.

He was in the wrong lane, merging the front end of his vehicle towards Alice's driver's side. In moments, the life within her, once reeling with the thought of the time soon to come, was vanquished as she lay, motionless.

The man behind the other wheel encountered a similar fate and his body, devoid of essence, was found awkwardly positioned over a single large shard of glass that still remained of his windshield.

Within the Haskell residence, the commotion only few feet away, could be heard with ghastly detail. Every terrible movement defined itself in such a way that even though Peter insisted Sarah stay inside with her brother intending to protect him from whatever would be discovered as the source, all, even Martin, were certain the cause.

"Alice!"

Martin screamed and ripped beyond Sarah who gave chase, but could do very little to impede the man. Peter could do even less as Martin sped by him nearly knocking him over.

The couple called out for Martin, but in moments, he was at the accident site. With a few powerful heaves, Martin ripped the metal debris inhibiting access to his beloved. Holding Alice in his arms as he sat on the asphalt, Martin wept and continuously repeated one word, the only word he would ever say again, "Alice."

Peter and Sarah could only watch in horror.

An hour passed before the authorities finally arrived and nearly every member made an attempt to withdraw Alice from Martin's grasp. Sarah and Peter made great efforts to convince Martin that he needed to let her go and several strange men even attempted to restrain him. If the grasp was to be opened, it would only be by Martin's will. Finally it was, as four paramedics were allowed to retrieve the body and Martin was left staring into his empty hands, with his eyes no longer seeing, ears no longer hearing and mind no longer composed.

Several more hours passed as Martin remained in the road fixated; withdrawn from everything, even Sarah, who remained as Peter followed the others to handle the required paperwork. Several lightly offered words were not heard by Martin, and were barely spoken through tears by Sarah. At one point, she attempted to caress her brother's shoulder in hopes that this would ease him into a loving embrace. Instead, he lurched away...and ran.

Sarah chased and called out to her brother once more. After some time spent chasing she became exhausted and collapsed to a grassy floor. With her head planted in the grass and her hands desperately digging into the soil, she quaked as every emotion she collected throughout her life seemed to bellow out through strained screams.

Martin kept running long into the night. He could hardly see the world before him and paid no mind to what lay behind. He ran hoping his legs would give out and his body would simply die. He was so confused and lost within his own mind that he would not even be aware.

He did fall; down the side of a short cliff just beside a highway, until his body had finally been freed of momentum. Just before his mind closed from consciousness, he was placed in his own shoes as a child, running through the Bitterroot Pines carrying a lifeless body; it was at once both Sarah and Alice. His screams made no sound to give either one a name.

Four days later found Martin in a hospital bed, with his sister watching over him in a position she had never hoped to find herself. Peter was with them and for each, every moment crept by in agony. Martin was awake, but he was not speaking. His staring eyes would not move, and to touch him received the same response one would expect when touching the bark of a tree.

Eventually, the physical wounds healed and Martin was released. With Sarah and Peter at either side, he was led away from his room. To see him walk was to watch the movement of a machine; rigid, sterile with no evidence that any thought was being committed.

He returned home with Peter and Sarah, but he did not return to work, or to any previous routine. They, with the occupation of time being their only escape, returned to the clinic and made desperate attempts to resume a life that seemed forever lost. Martin resigned himself to his room. He ate seldom, drank little, and spoke no words. It was only through medication that he was able to sleep.

Time passed relentlessly with despair in the Haskell home. Sarah and Peter improved with the support of one another, but no effort, no matter how thoroughly applied on Martin's behalf, found any improvement in the man's demeanor. He was there, but only physically so.

"Martin, please...please, come sit with us in the visiting room. Peter's put on your favorite album. He even said he'd dance with you..."

A chuckle, choked slightly with tears was spent in vain. Martin sat upright on his bed staring out his window, motionless.

"Please Martin. We love you. It's killing me to see you like this..."

Martin stood up and Sarah watched in amazement, nearly smiling as she reluctantly allowed herself to hope. He turned to his credenza and retrieved a sheet of paper and pencil, then began to draw frantically. He looked up to Sarah and she smiled. He stopped drawing, pointed to the door, and waited.

Tears welled in Sarah's eyes once more as she exited his room, closing the door behind her. She fell to the floor and held her face, weeping for a few minutes until she was retrieved by Peter. He led her away from Martin's room, down the flight of stairs and into the kitchen where he offered her his attempt at her scone recipe.

"I botched it, but I think some parts are salvageable."

With a stupid grin, Peter drew a smile from his wife just before embracing her.

Martin continued tearing along the paper's surface in a frenzied state as he emptied everything his mind would allow. This continued for two hours until he stopped abruptly, dropping the paper and pencil to the floor and with his mind clear for just one moment, he leapt through his bedroom window.

As he fell, he closed his eyes and retreated to the vacancy he'd created within his mind.

The shattering glass rattled the two in the kitchen and both raced up the stairs. Peter threw the door open and Sarah vaulted to the window. She turned her head away instantly and bellowed.

"Martin!"

On the floor, held up by arms fixed straight and parallel, Sarah hung her head and forced her eyes closed as tight as her contorted face would allow.

Peter, torn between running to comfort his wife and running to find the body of Martin, instead stood in the doorway, dumbfounded.

Sarah opened her eyes and just below her head, visible in the shadow she cast, she saw the image Martin so fervently evacuated from his thoughts. A thicket of chaos and noise, so immense it was nearly solid black broke away in its center and seemed to retreat from a heavenly glow protecting a shape, a form Sarah recognized as her brother. The glow with its shaded recesses and contours made another familiar shape, a woman, surrounding and holding Martin within and keeping the darkness at bay. It was both Sarah and Alice and it was all Martin ever hoped to convey to either of them, but could never find the words.

TO BE LOST OUTSIDE

Curious, they keep digging up landmines.
I'm worried they're going to explode.
They think they're searching for diatribes,
Or some secret that needs to be told.

But oh, if they only knew,
The lampoons these stories grow.
The pages are dripping with a manifest,
Of the things we aren't meant to know.

And yes, I have seen one of those,
And I wish that I had been blind.
To sate by way of the undisclosed,
Is to corrupt an innocent mind.

To say there's a bliss found in ignorance,
May condemn a desire for truth.
But yes, there is safety in shelter,
And an envy of innocent youth.

BEASTS OF BURDEN

Four years passed after the Great War, and the small isolated town of Rubstoyevka, finds it has inherited some of the worst traits much of the country of Russia has suffered as a result of the terrible strife. Inhabited by the horribly impoverished; a meager and malnourished population, and some of the most unforgiving winters ever recorded. A butcher finds his business in dire straits in this poor town, and watches as his friends and loved ones slowly succumb to the daunting climate and the resulting starvation.

This butcher, Kirill Pushkin, previously left his life and business behind when he was called upon to join as a sharpshooter and serve his country in the greatest conflict it had ever seen. After returning once the war had ended, or possibly suspended momentarily, he reinitiated his small shop and was moderately successful, if only for a few years. During the third year following his return, a harsh and relentless winter began and an outbreak of typhus struck the town of Rubstoyevka, as well as the surrounding areas. During this time of arctic temperatures, severe blizzards and horrible epidemic, Pushkin lost nearly all of his livestock and was left with only one steed, just strong and young enough to brave the climate. His shop, his bins and his ice boxes, he found to be largely vacant, bearing only those meager and undesirable cuts that remained unsold. Of the withered and deprived pig carcasses that remained, the scantly edible meat could only be stretched so far, and for so long.

The isolated town of Rubstoyevka remained, after the spread of disease and the bouts with severe winter, with a vastly dwindling population of villagers composed primarily of women, children and the elderly. Of the few able and strong men not lost to the war, none had any true means of transportation, save for Kirill's thinning horse and his brother Nyekev's aging, petrol-less and often unreliable pickup. No villagers could be expected to brave the overpowering, harsh climate and manage travel to find a means of survival or assistance elsewhere. Importation, as yet another resulting misfortune, had been out of the question for quite some time, insuring that any such means of sustainability were not only scarce within the town itself, but were indeed, nonexistent. Rubstoyevka could no longer support itself and seemed only capable of dystrophic collapse. It was as if some great malicious entity had risen with the winter, only to entrap them with the unrelenting storm, forcing their bondage.

Kirill had, of course, found his business to be entirely unprofitable, relying on trade and promises in exchange for cuts of meat. This, to Kirill, was of no consequence. What concerned him was the town's complete reliance on him as their primary source of sustenance, of which he had none. He felt a heavy burden, watching the town's descent as its people became increasingly malnourished. He believed strongly that it was up to him, being one of the most capable of the few men remaining in the town, to be the bearer of the burden. Though at the onset he had no idea what he would do, he still gladly accepted the task of providing the town the food they required.

The butcher shop was closed on this particular day, as Kirill had decided it best to set aside the time to consider possible solutions, in hopes that at least one may present itself. In the cooling room, nearly completely vacant, save for two boars, Kirill sat on a small crate stroking the well-tempered blade of his most dependable carving knife and pondered the possible actions that could be taken to save his shop, himself, and at the forefront of his concerns, the town.

The first thought to arrest his troubled mind, revolved slowly and painfully around his only remaining, and most faithful horse, Indrik. Even in such desperate times as these, Kirill knew he would sooner give himself as provision than to offer the flesh of his loyal friend. He then expanded upon the thought of human consumption, with the idea of a sacrifice of certain members of the town in order to nourish others, allowing them to endure, until the climate improved and they could again travel and seek support. Kirill even considered the truth that the villagers would not likely be directly opposed to this, as they were, perhaps, even more desperate than he. However, the suffering and adversity the town had already overcome, Kirill knew, would have been in vain if they were to resort to manslaughter and cannibalism. These ideas, he couldn't allow himself to entertain any longer. He shook his head, as if releasing the disparaging thoughts in the process.

Instead, he nurtured the consideration of wildlife in the surrounding area. Of this, to his knowledge, there was likely very little, as most of the fauna had thinned to passing or had merely left with instinctual predictions of the troubling climate to come. However, what did remain, could indeed, be hunted. The woods were roughly seventy kilometers outside of the town along a desolate and barren road; it would be an arduous task for him to brave the weather. He would need to take Indrik with him, and between them share the burden. Kirill wondered if Indrik would be up to the task. As it is, there is so little meat, Kirill would need to make a weighty haul in order to last just a few days. He and Indrik would need to share the burden along what would likely be a harsh, cold and unforgiving trek. Kirill knew he could bear the journey and several more, but Indrik was young and losing strength with each passing day as he had been stabled too long, and should something happen to the poor colt, Kirill would not only be devastated, but surely stranded. However, Kirill realized he could find no other option, and he would rather die trying to make a noble effort than stay and resort to the lifestyle of a savage. If Indrik could speak, Kirill thought, he would most certainly agree.

With a light relief of consternation, Kirill Pushkin stood and sighed. He was relieved that, at the very least, he was no longer in the dark. He had a plan. Though as a simple plan, it was far from foolproof, success would not be implausible. It couldn't be, as a last ditch effort; it was all he had. With his carving knife in hand, Pushkin began stripping meat from the two remaining pork carcasses in the freezer and gathered what remains he had of feed and produce. He and Indrik would need to eat a hearty dinner that night and he would need to prepare enough meat, in addition to what remained of the few crops and feed not lost to the freeze, to allow for what could possibly be a four or five day excursion. He decided that he would need to salt and smoke roughly two kilograms of pork overnight to last through the trip. This night he would prepare the head, jowl, ears, tail and hooves of both bodies. These parts would be the least desirable, and should he return with nothing he would at least have two full pork bodies to offer.

That night Pushkin ate his hearty dinner of stew, bread rations and fatty gravy and the young and maturing Indrik dined upon carrot pieces, hay, pork scraps and grain. Before retiring for the night, Pushkin cleaned and readied his rifle which he attached to Indrik's saddle accompanying a lantern, a satchel of ammunition, a can of kerosene, a canteen of water, the skins of four large grey wolves his father trapped, sewn together for sleeping, a pipe, some old, but strong red pipe tobacco he had acquired during the war, and an ever useful bottle of vodka. He had also found several trapping nets to use to haul whatever, if anything, he catches. On his back, he would carry another satchel, which he packed what remained of his bread rations, matches, and a few potatoes and carrots with room still for his renowned smoked pork.

Once Indrik was comfortably asleep, Kirill left his shop and walked westward along the main road to his brother Nyekev's house. Nyekev was something of the town's mayor, if unofficially so, and was also the only person who shared the knowledge of Kirill's diminished stock. He and Kirill both agreed that the town should not be made aware, as it would only depress them further and likely cause irreparable damage from the resulting desperation. Knocking on the door, Kirill was relieved to be met by his brother and not his wife. It was late, and it would be difficult for him to explain himself to someone not in the know, so to speak. Nyekev was not surprised to see his brother and in fact, had stayed awake into the late night, expecting him. He invited Kirill in and they both sat at the table, each with a small glass of his brother's favorite spirit, a sixteen year old Belgian Jenever. Nyekev informed his younger brother that it was safe to speak as his wife and daughters were fast asleep.

So the Pushkin's shared a brief discussion and half of the bottle of gin before Nyekev had agreed to manage the shop for the next few days under the pretense that Kirill had been stricken with a contagious illness and was being cared for by the local physician, Alek Porkiev, who being of stable mind, would be able to accept the true circumstances and manage the shared facade.

The next morning Kirill awoke with a great amount of excitement and perseverance. Though anxious, he was looking forward to the trip; to the exhilaration of pitting himself against immense odds and testing his stamina, constitution and abilities once more. He wondered if Indrik felt the same. He too was already awake, early at sunrise, and Kirill being able to read the horse's subtle expressions very well, suspected strongly that Indrik knew they were leaving, perhaps, never to return. With Indrik's somewhat greedy help, Kirill finished what remained of the dinner prepared the short night before. Afterwards, Kirill retrieved the adequate slabs of pork from his outside smoker and wrapped them in wax paper and tin foil, packing them in his satchel. On his person he bore a long leather coat, covering two wool sweaters, and long underwear strapped with the satchel, his carving knife, and another water canteen. He affixed Indrik with a small basin and his loaded saddle and mounted the horse.

The road could be accessed from the south end of Kirill's several acres of now frozen and largely barren land. This, Kirill was thankful for, as it meant he would not have to traverse through the town and be forced to answer questions as to where he was proceeding and what he had planned.

Indrik carried his master with surprising aptitude for the first twenty kilometers before stopping. Though the sky had cleared momentarily for the first time in months that fateful morning, this translucency was short lived and the fierce clouds once again obscured every aspect of the sky throwing great shadows over the path which was blanketed with nearly one meter of snow. Indrik had been stabled for a great duration and was expected to require frequent stops. In this instance however, Pushkin initiated the stop, and did so with the reins held long and his heels pressed into Indrik's sides, knowing full well that his loyal companion would gallop into the throes of death with his master encumbering his every step.

With hands on the reins, Pushkin guided his stallion off the path into a small clearing where he dismounted and retrieved his water canteen. After pouring a small amount into the basin, he waited patiently as Indrik guzzled the water. Pushkin then inspected his horse and found a slight spasm in Indrik's right hind leg. He massaged it and applied an analgesic salve Alek had prepared for him. He did this with the insistence he would use it frequently to deter the various aches and pains that come with age. Pushkin had never once used it himself, but knowing the brunt of the work would be accomplished by Indrik and the least he could do would be to ensure his steed was as able and comfortable as possible. An hour passed as they lingered in a small, shallow clearing resting upon Pushkin's wolf skins splayed out over the snow and also covering the still bodies before Pushkin had decided it was time to continue. He had hoped they would not need to rest again until they reached the outer edges of the forest.

By the time forty kilometers had developed behind the venturing man and his mount, a great blizzard of determined and heavy snow began to insist they retreat, and though it did so fervently, it found only disobedience in the equally determined travelers. Pushkin braved the weather wrapped from head to toe in wolf fur with the remaining fur armoring Indrik's face and hind. The small portion of Pushkin's face left peering through the pelt became numb and bright red as his blood vessels constricted and dilated. The temperature had dropped considerably in the past hour and the two, now very weary travelers, found themselves almost incapable of progressing any further. Pushkin decided to lead off the increasingly obscured path and, with Indrik's assistance, slowly searched through the inhospitable surroundings for any kind of landmark visible enough to direct their travel. In a short distance, Pushkin could make out what appeared to be a very large and very out-of-place tree. With a flick of the reins he guided his steed in the direction of the tree.

As they grew near, the tree became increasingly vast and Pushkin took note of its remarkably odd shape. It was akin to no other tree he had ever seen. The seemingly thousands of limbs grew almost suddenly from only the very top of the tree. Some of the limbs climbed upwards and outwards, but most slithered down almost parallel to the tree's trunk, as if reaching below to the tree's roots. It bore many eerily shaped long slender leaves as well. Once he was within only twenty meters of the tree, Pushkin could attest that the leaves were blue, appearing like long, dark and sinister icicles suspended from the limbs. The tree stood untouched by the snow, and there was no accumulation in the canopy as was the case with every other large floral lifeform of the forest. He considered for a moment, the ominous nature of the somehow otherworldly tree that stood with such grand significance that even the weather refrained from disrupting its disquieting majesty. Pushkin shuddered. Had they not had such a great need for some form of shelter, he would have opted to continue on and leave the foreboding, if not macabre tree to haunt its worrisome clearing alone.

The air and atmosphere grew warmer and cleared as the two slowly and reluctantly neared the trunk. Pushkin could feel the blood begin to circulate again in his face as the air regained a bearable temperature. Indrik, which had previously been completely averse to continue towards the tree, requiring considerable provocation, now seemed to also welcome the new comfort of the heated environment surrounding the strange timbered growth.

About a meter from the tree trunk, Pushkin halted his horse and climbed down to the dry, dirt floor. The ground immediately around the tree's trunk was bare and the soil ghostly white. In the close vicinity of the tree, the air was acrid with a pungent odor Pushkin could not place, but immediately detested. He reached out with his hand and once it had extended only centimeters from the tree, he immediately jerked it back in bewildered amusement. The tree was radiating immense heat and its surface was far too searing to even touch. More signs to indicate an unnatural abomination that would typically send Indrik and even Pushkin running, but these conditions were ignored. Indrik crept closer to the tree and stopped, seeming to be content with his current surroundings. Pushkin removed his gloves and placed them on the dirt floor near the base of the trunk and held his hands warming them near the tree's stark white surface as if they were embracing the heat of a fire. Indirk took his place beside Pushkin and knelt to the base of the trunk. He pushed aside some of the light soil with his muzzle and uprooted a small fungal growth, preparing to eat it. Pushkin quickly retrieved the strange illuminated blue mushroom from the steed's mouth and tossed it aside, surprised not only by the ease with which the horse had found the morsel, but that something emitting such a foul stench would be considered delectable to the beast.

"Foolish Indrik. Nothing of this tree can be good for us; we really should not be here."

Putting to words his unease, Kirill's feelings persisted; that this abominable growth should be avoided at all costs. Kirill found himself embattled between the oddly alluring comfort provided by the tree, and the sheer terror its very presence seemed to instill deep within him.

After only a few minutes passing, Kirill's focus shifted suddenly. Just outside of the perimeter bathed in a blue glow emitted from the tree, he had caught a glimpse of something speeding by. Perceptibly on all fours, it passed by in the distance heading to the east, and from the quick indecisive glimpse Kirill was afforded, it appeared to have been alone. Kirill retrieved his rifle from his saddle and cocked it, ensuring the chamber was readied. With its indistinct image reforming in his mind, it began to take the shape of a large boar or something very similar. As odd as its presence seemed to be, he had weighed the thought against that of a blue-leaved and lustrous tree and considered it nearly common. If he'd found boar, it would be a godsend; with this tempting thought Kirill returned to his feet.

Three more figures formed through the thick, hoary air and no sooner than he had taken stance, the other which had raced by moments before, returned and joined the group. They were nearing and seemed to be proceeding towards the hunter. They became clear as they advanced, revealing their details. Kirill could see now; they were not boars. They were horrendous and malformed, bearing thick leathery skin pocked with convex brown growths and randomly scattered patches of coarse black hair. Their viscous white eyes, of which he could make out four to each beast, protruded on each side of the head and were of various sizes and positions, with no symmetry to speak of. Each had a muzzle which ended in a sharp beak-like protuberance that meshed seamlessly into several large tusks. In place of ears were short perforations, surrounded by sagging fleshy lobes. They could have only resembled boars in scant fleeting glimpses.

The bodies raced along on three legs, two malformed and stunted hind legs and one fore leg located below the nape of the creature's neck. They operating in a massive amalgam of muscle and flesh jutting from the barreled chests of the few aberrations. Instead of hooves, the legs ended in sharp claw-like stumps.

He could hear them, squelching out hurried and alarming sounds which rang in Kirill's mind as the cries of pain and angst. Without hesitation, Kirill let out a single shot striking one of the swine mockeries in the center of the head, effectively ceasing its apparent suffering. The remaining trio retreated in all directions and disappeared into the cold blizzard. Braving the cold and leaving the circle of warmth circumventing the tree, Kirill approached the felled corpse. As he neared, through the several layers of hides and cloth wrapped around his face, Kirill was assaulted with the dead being's all but overwhelming stench. If he had not just watched the creature die, he would have thought it had become severely rancid after weeks of decay. Though almost unbearable, even for a veteran butcher, he fought through the rank odor and knelt down closer to the lifeless mass, grabbing the legs and hoisting the foul and heavy body over his shoulders.

He returned to the tree's bank and laid the beast out beside Indrik, who took a few steps back, shook his head and snorted, in an apparent response to the odor. Shaking his head once more, Indrik then let out a cry of what could only be described as utter repulsion. Kirill stroked the horse's mane and settled him some before removing a few ropes wrapped around the saddle. He proceeded to tie the beast's hind and forelegs together, fashioned a strap and hoisted the creature to the back of Indrik's saddle. This appeared to cause the horse chagrin, as he kicked some and again shook his head, but ever the loyal servant, Indrik settled and accepted the added weight.

"I hope this won't be too much for you boy, but I promise you a feast when we return—of what, however, I cannot say. At least, it won't be mushrooms." Indrik did not appear to find his master's words very reassuring.

Kirill reclaimed his position atop Indrik's saddle, gave his friend a light, but stern heel-kick and Indrik responded with a well-paced gallop. As they hurried off, not entirely certain of their direction, two of the creatures approached the tree as they had done many times before, pressed their beaks into the ground around its trunk and proceeded to rifle through the soil.

They travelled quickly through the snow in what they had estimated, or hoped, to be their origin. After placing a few dozen meters between them and the perverse tree, Kirill spotted another quickly moving shape in the distance to his left. Redirecting his focus, he saw the creature's form more clearly and recognized it to be another one of the oddities; the peculiar boar-like beasts from before. With its quick movement, Kirill feared any time devoted to stopping and dismounting would be too costly, and retrieved his rifle. Having never fired from horseback, Kirill's confidence faltered some, but his aim did not. Shortly after the crack of the gunshot, the quickly moving shadow in the distance slowed to a crawl before collapsing. Kirill flicked the reins and redirected their path of travel.

Dismounting, Kirill had almost lost his footing as a strong burst of wind blasted and staggered through the forest. The storm was getting worse and Kirill realized quickly that they must hurry if they are to make it back in such escalating conditions. He hesitated for a moment and considered leaving the second carcass where it lay rather than increasing his poor friend's burden; but to lose any meat to scavengers or the elements during such times would be a travesty. He hoisted up the body just as before and strapped it to the other side of the saddle, hoping to at least balance Indrik's additional cargo.

Mounting the horse once more, Kirill attempted to spur Indrik's side, but making very clear his desires to linger no longer, Indrik raced off at full gallop before Kirill even landed his heel. The man steadied his position and fastened his hands tightly around the reins, with adrenaline surging through him in response to Indrik's incredible burst of speed.

Both parties silently agreed that there should be no further stops for rest; only a mad dash for home. Every step found Indrik fiercely battling the great blasts of frozen wind, but he continued to push forward with all of the strength he could muster. Kirill wished more could be done to assist his horse. The only way he could think to help was to lean down close to horse's nape and make himself, and thus Indrik, less resistant to the wind. In this manner they proceeded for two hours, growing more concerned by the minute with their choice in direction.

Nearing the end of the second hour, Kirill began to see, albeit vaguely in the thick, white air, the small lit lantern posts leading to his gate. Indrik maintained his feverish pace and rushed through the few acres between the gate and the covered enclosure leading to the back of Kirill's house and butcher shop.

Kirill dismounted quickly, and hurriedly removed the loads bearing down far too greatly upon Indrik's swollen muscles. After setting the saddle and carcasses aside, Kirill proceeded to massage Indrik and checked his legs, ensuring there were no signs of swelling or strain. Indrik revealed no duress and appeared only to need rest. Kirill patted the horse briefly and sighed in relief. To have Indrik become lame would have been about all he could bare.

Entering his house, Pushkin began stocking the fireplace with Indrik waiting beside him expectantly. With the fire lit and quickly building the well-needed heat, he retrieved the carcasses and what remained of the stock tied to the saddle.

He hauled the carcasses into his makeshift cooling room, and begins inspecting the bodies. The hideous carcasses were no longer emitting the strong scent of rot as they had just after being felled, and though initially concerned with the potential for disease in the meat, the smell had become so similar to that of game boar, he had hunted in years past, the worry softened. Pushkin proceeded to inspection, opening the mouths and checking the many strange, thin and sharp teeth arranged in three rows along both the upper and lower jaws. The gums appeared healthy, providing their pink, fleshy support around each secured tooth. The tongues, though considerably smaller than that of an average boar, raised no concerns; their texture, and color, with the saliva appearing mostly clear and appropriate in viscosity.

Pushkin then lifted the lids surrounding the several, awkwardly positioned eyes and found the skin to bear the proper coloring around the eyes, but the eyes themselves appeared completely black with no sclera to speak of. After gently pressing his finger into one of the eyes, a semi-transparent membrane retracted and reveals the eye to be even darker than he had originally perceived, with traces of red ligaments radiating from the barely apparent pupil.

Pushkin gently probed along the ribcage, spine and undercarriage of each body; no swelling or bruising could be found and the bodies felt remarkably warm in the freezing temperatures of the room. Fine patches of hair were firmly planted along the dark leathery hide of each corpse. To their touch, Pushkin found the hairs to be incredibly rigid for their size and resembling porcupine quills in their tendency to remain attached to his hand as if hooked or barbed at the tips. Pushkin jerked his hand back and sure enough, several of the quills remained attached to his palm. Using a set of calipers, he removed them and briefly observed the small indentation the quills left in his hand.

Though the carcasses were certainly strange and dissimilar in many ways to anything he had ever found in the forest, Pushkin found them to be, at the very least, healthy. Once butchered, he had hoped they would provide, if even in small amounts, suitable meat to distribute to Rubstoyevka.

Leaving the carcasses in the cooling room, and Indrik comfortably resting before the fireplace, Kirill quietly proceeded to his brother's home, hoping the darkening sky and snow-filled air would obscure him enough that he may avoid encounters with others of town in the short trek. Nyekev, once again, greeted the younger of the Pushkin brothers at the door and invited him in. Regaled with the story of his brother's incredible adventure, Nyekev was ever grateful for his younger's safe return. Unfortunately, the tale he had received from Kirill was fictionalized, as though Kirill was not fond of providing such mistruths to his brother, he was apprehensive at his possible reception of the inexplicable truth.

In his recount, the outlandish tree was replaced by a fire he had only barely managed to set and maintain only briefly, using bundles of straw as a temporary shelter. The once odd and unnamed creatures had become simple wild boars, apparently living out of their element in a desperate response for survival. All other details were merely avoided and the adventure was only harrowing in the most predictable respects. Still, Nyekev was satisfied and the Pushkin's toasted to not only this, but all safe returns.

After some time spent enjoying the company of his brother and his family, Kirill returned home. Here he found no surprises; the house was comfortably warmed and Indrik seemed to be enjoying the restful atmosphere of heated familiarity. Kirill retreated to the cooling room after ensuring Indrik had been fed what remained of his prepared stock. Here too, he found no surprises. The carcasses were placed along his tables, awaiting the process of skinning; one which Kirill, admittedly, was hesitant to perform.

He began with the first body on its back placed over his slick covered table, splitting open the midriff with a lengthy incision. Having opened the body, he was perplexed with the sight. The lungs appeared considerably malformed and rested as two small, misshaped organs within the unusually spherical ribcage. The heart, conversely, was far larger than any he had seen in his years as a butcher. Strange in its long shape, the heart ran between two stomachs, parallel to the spine. Intestinal tracks pulled aside revealed only one kidney. A liver apparently divided into interconnected quadrants, accompanied three other organs, which Kirill could only surmise to be bladders.

Many of the organs removed were stored in preserving liquids. These would only be useful in ground forms or sausages, as Kirill expects a liver malformed and split with ventricular cavities would be an unappetizing and confusing sight. Again, Kirill considered the nature of the beasts and hesitated, but with the organs healthy, odd though they were, he could see no perceivable harm in their consumption.

He continued. Drying the emptied cavity, Kirill proceeded to identifying the cuts. Difficulty arose in the search for the shoulders and loins, as the bizarrely shaped body formed around the support of three oddly-positioned legs, but the general rule of thirds for each bodily section seemed to apply. The ribs, loins and shoulder meats would require little treatment to their appearance if cut properly. The body was quite large and could be spread thin and still manage to amply feed the dwindling town. Eight swift strikes of his heavy cleaver were required to remove the head. No pig ever required such effort and upon close inspection Kirill could see the source of difficulty. A massive single vertebra, now halved with the cleaver, spanned nearly the entire length of the neck, which was evidentially not intended to feature any sort of flexibility. The bone marrow, so dense within, could be boiled into a feast all its own. After pondering and internally remarking on the many peculiarities to be found with the creature, Kirill gracefully and precisely halved the remainder of the pig and scoured its hide removing the outer-most layer of skin, along with the strange quill patches. He marked the body and head and determined a variety of fifteen cuts could be successfully produced from the carcass. After having cut the body into three manageable portions, he stored them along with the head to be cut the following morning. The second carcass, Kirill scoured, split in half and hung on a meat hook suspended from the cooling room's ceiling.

After finishing his work for the night, Kirill decided to cook a small portion of a shoulder cut for his evening meal. He simply roasted this over the open flame of his fireplace and prepared a halved potato and a glass of red wine he had saved from the war. Indrik was watching with intense curiosity. Kirill tasted, with slight reluctance, the first fork-full of the odd, unidentifiable creatures. As his teeth relentlessly ripped and tenderized the meat, the juices escaped and coated in small currents along his tongue introducing the full flavor to his palette. He had expected the unmistakable taste of game, possibly tainted, instead the flavor was remarkably savory and rich, and though it certainly resembled pork in its salty succulence, it was far more flavorful with a pleasing hint of sweetness and the delicate tenderness of veal. Had he not seen the grotesque beasts in all their form, based purely on taste, he would have envisioned something entirely unlike the three-legged monstrosities.

Unexpectedly satisfied with the meal, Kirill followed with the celebratory glass of wine and retired for the night.

The morning that followed was momentous. Kirill, excited to greet the town and the day for the first time in many years, began early with the work of a butcher. He had prepared an assortment of cuts, retrieved the remainder of his smoked pork and packaged as much as could be comfortably packed in Indrik's saddle bags. During this period of great preparation, Indrik enjoyed a grand meal of hay and grain and was treated to several carrots, as a big day awaited him, just as it did his master.

Riding through the still frozen and winded town, the two proceeded door-to-door and face-to-face with every member of the small town of Rubstoyevka. Each were greeted with a week's worth of meat, prepared several ways; as sausages, famously smoked pork briskets, finely ground meat—some seasoned and unseasoned, and finally, some preserved in jars waiting to be pickled. The greatest of smiles never once ceased on Kirill's face as he gladly diminished the entire stock of the two large bodies with just enough spare himself to portion. Through a few select days surrounding those he would otherwise, supply with potatoes and carrots. He cared not for what he would lack, as it meant the town would finally be stocked once more, in its time of greatest need.

After a very long day of preparing and delivering the meat, the two returned home just after nightfall as exhausted as the night before, but all the more satisfied with the day's work. Indrik was simply pleased with the riding. It had been too long since he had been out of the house and stable, and in the last two days, he had more than made up for it. Kirill, with his horse, dined more moderately that night and turned to rest with stomachs full, but not bloated. Rubstoyevka's other residents could not say the same, for many of the town engorged themselves with meat-laden feasts befitting kings.

Another morning found the skies burdened with snow, fiercely pummeling everything into obscurity. Kirill woke to the sound of pounding at his door with a mild ache in his stomach, perhaps in anxious response to the summons at such an early hour. Answering the door he found a couple standing before him with great expectations gleaming in their eyes; a townsperson by the name of Vladimir and his wife, Mila. They informed him that in a single night, they, their three children, Vladimir's mother, Mila's brother and cousin, and their dog had consumed all but one quarter of the meat they were gifted. Though they had no way of paying or even bartering for additional meat, nor indeed the meat they were given, they demanded more. Kirill simply had not realized so many were sharing the same roof, and though initially taken aback by the brazen demands and wanton gluttony, he felt as though he may well have shorted them unintentionally. With this in mind, he invited the couple inside and asked their patience as he left to retrieve what remained of his portion.

"I am terribly sorry for this, but unfortunately, what you see before you is all that remains of what has been butchered. Please take this, and tomorrow I should have more prepared."

Vladimir having watched closely as his wife's face turned to one of dismay responded,

"This will not suffice. We must have more. We have a very large family and many mouths to feed. If need be, I will assist you in butchering."

Vladimir, sparing little concern for his intrusion, attempted to enter Kirill's cooling room. He was immediately halted by the large and formidably statured butcher, who was experiencing far more than exasperation, as his stomach pains became heightened greatly by the confrontation.

"I must insist that you accept what I have given you and take your leave. I ensure you, I will have more by midday tomorrow. Please, you must make this last in the meantime."

Mila then spoke up in a hurried, anxious and unyielding tone,

"Midday tomorrow? Surely you are joking. This simply will not do. My children have been starving, and finally when we have something to eat, it is such a meager amount. Why will you not allow my husband to assist you? What are you hiding?"

Indeed, Kirill was hiding the remains of the bodies as he feared he could never explain them in any palatable way to the intruders. Still, he was shocked by the implication and it seemed a desperation had pushed them from a once friendly demeanor to one of belligerence; he improvised his response,

"Butchering is no simple task. I would appreciate the help, but I fear such great effort and time would be required in the instruction that the meat would be no sooner prepared than were I to continue alone. And though I mean no offense, it may even be a hindrance. After I have prepared more for your family tomorrow and the town is well-stocked for the days to come, I would gladly accept your husband's assistance, if the offer is to remain."

Kirill grasped the man's shoulder gently and gestured to the door. "Please. Tomorrow. I assure you, you will receive your fair share of provisions. I only ask that you make due for a short time with what little I have prepared."

Mila harbored no intention of refraining, and in fact, was about to erupt into a frenzy. Vladimir, however, knew better of the circumstance, grasped his wife, nodded his head to the dining table burdened with Kirill's offering and presented her a stern expression. She responded, retrieving the cuts of meat, and followed her husband to the door.

"I sincerely hope you and your family can make the best of this small offering. May you all fare well today, and I will greet you again tomorrow with a banquet."

Kirill offered a smile, both sincere and wearied, but received no response in kind. The couple left his house in sullen silence.

Kirill knew he must return to the forest and hunt the beasts once more. However, before this, he would need to scour every inch of his cooling room and leave no trace of the carcasses, burning what remained of the entrails and burying the bones. After some time spent in this process, Kirill had finally finished and left riding Indrik.

He had hoped that his brother would assist him in tending to his shop in his absence once more. How long this could proceed he did not know, but surmised that matters would become very difficult in times to come, and hoped greatly that the storm would let up before this should be the case.

Returning to Nyekev's home once more, later in the already troubling day, Kirill was greeted by his brother's wife, Dominika. After she explained that Nyekev had taken ill, Kirill followed her to his brother's room, with his stomach churning and quaking, even more so after being assaulted with the musk of disease and decay blanketing the room.

"Brother, it seems the epidemic isn't behind us after all."

Dominika, clearly despondent, left the room in tears, following her husband's words as Kirill removed his cap and sat beside his bedridden brother.

"Don't say that Nyekev."

Kirill watched as his brother clutched his stomach tightly with a grimace. As an apparent fever burned in red through his face, Kirill stared at Nyekev's skin gleaming in the low lantern light with a copious amount of sweat. Under this reflected coating of perspiration, he could see that his brother was developing protuberances and small sores along the side of his face.

"It can't be Typhus, it—whatever it is, it will pass. Get rest brother and Dominika will tend to you, nursing you back to health. After all, she's saved you once before."

Kirill smiled and forced a brief chuckle. Nyekev, to his brother's slight relief, responded in kind.

"Yes…yes I do feel exhausted. However, if it does not pass very soon, I may ask that you return that favor brother, and lead the town in my stead."

"It will not come to that, Nyekev. Sleep now and tomorrow will find you well."

Kirill found Dominika in the kitchen and asked how she and her children fared. They managed very well and were remarking only the night before how blessed they were to have their health and a brother and uncle to provide such an abundance of fine meat. She added, in response to Kirill's following question, over three-quarters remained. Kirill was relieved to hear this, as the thought of having given his brother tainted meat had crossed his mind, but as they had not consumed much and the others in town seemed to be experiencing no similar symptoms, he surmised his brother must be ailing in some other way, he'd certainly hoped his own words were true, and it was not Typhus. Kirill left, admitting to himself that it was too much to bear to see his brother in such a state, and his efforts, only those that would have any meaning, would be best spent in keeping the town and his ailing brother nourished.

No Pushkin would be tending the shop that day. Instead, Kirill finished preparing, locked the doors and left his house vacant as he and Indrik set out to venture into the forest once more, this time with an even greater burden wearing upon Kirill's heart and mind. It reminded him, with the assistance of his stomach, even in those brief moments when he had managed to follow another train of thought.

Before entering the forest, Kirill rode with great reluctance through the town. A thought weighing heavily in his mind, he set a destination he wished he could have avoided. He might have left for the hunt, and had certainly intended to, convincing himself that he could return with more meat and that all would be well. But with his stomach aching so much, he could scarcely bare it and he was constantly reminded of a concern deeply troubling him.

It had been nearly a year since last Kirill had seen Vladimir's home at the foothills of mount Rubstoyevka. It was not likely many outside of the Shursky family themselves traveled the path of late. Vladimir often took it upon himself to trek into town should they require any goods or services, but the way to the Shursky home was as recognizable as ever and as Kirill neared the home, he was almost comforted in the simple familiarity of the ride. Whatever unusual sights he was expecting to find could not be as terrible as his thoughts insisted, not with everything persisting such as it had for so many years. Kirill dismounted at the front door and immediately after, Indrik took several steps back. Kirill's comfort left him as suddenly as it had arrived.

Pushkin rapped gently on the door, but received no answer. Repeating twice with the same results, he finally opened the door and shouted a greeting. No response. Pushkin looked in to find three deceased children lying, torn asunder, on the floor in a collection of what remained of their own interiors. Pushkin's previous expectations, though terrible, could not compare. In fact, even his worst thoughts paled to the sight, as did he. Pushkin wished to turn, mount the steed and flee, but instead, proceeded into the house, calling for Vladimir and Mila who he had seen in high health, albeit dispirited, only hours before.

For a brief moment, Pushkin stopped and glanced at the face of one of the young departed vessels and quickly removed his gaze after seeing all he could bare. It was Vladimir's first born; a boy. Pushkin wished he could remember his name, if only to pay him proper respect in thought. The boy presented a face pocked with open sores formed around bone-like growths. It was covered in blood, still fresh and glistening in the light of candles and oil lanterns. The blood pooled greatest around the boy's mouth; open and vacant save for few grotesquely misshapen teeth that ended in sharp points. He had no nose or cavities where a nose might have been. It was just a mass of swollen sores, reddened and profusely scarred skin. The eyes were nearly lost in mounds of swelling tissue pushing them back deeply into the boy's skull.

Only hours had passed since last he had seen the couple. Pushkin wondered that in this short time, had these children taken such grotesque, unfortunate turns, or had this happened before their parent's visit to his shop? He knew he would likely never know and greatly desired not to.

Vladimir was found in a smaller room, just down a short hall. Pushkin thought he saw Vladimir hunched over, gently rocking and weeping, but as Pushkin neared he found that clutched tightly in his arms was Mila. She looked much like the children; in a horrible state worse than death. Upon Vladimir's face, what little Pushkin could decipher from his quietly crouched stance, he could see what appeared to be portions of Mila, enmeshed within pockets of the man's deformed flesh. Pushkin turned in silence and crept quietly back down the hall and to the front door.

Pushkin climbed upon Indrik's saddle and kicked harshly. Indrik was not in need of any such motivation and burst into a gallop. He wished to return to his brother's place, in hopes that he may find the family in a better state, or even to return home, if only to be alone with thoughts that would not leave his mind. Instead, Indrik spirited along at an alarming rate into the forest, with Pushkin incapable of doing little more than holding the reins with one hand and clutching his stomach in excruciation with the other.

The trip to the tree, though plagued with the same unrelenting weather, required nearly half of the time it had previously. Indrik was not only competent, but seemed to be unfazed by the blizzard, reaching speeds which Pushkin had never known a horse to be capable. To Pushkin, it seemed logic meant less and less in the past few days. Were his thoughts not solely dedicated to his brother, spare those arrested by his stomach, he might have considered correlations outside of coincidence. He tried to focus only to have the thoughts that raced in condemnation through every possibility he may have wrought cause despair as his vision waned in great response to his abdominal pain.

They found the tree once more. Indrik more so than Pushkin, who was finding great difficulty in remaining with the moments at hand. Very little time had passed since last they had felt the tree's radiant warmth and yet it had grown extensively. The tree appeared to stand nearly three times greater than before and the snow cover halted at a radius roughly three-hundred meters from the tree's trunk. The limbs and branches were at once expanding to the sky and in some places descending downward where they connected with the trees exposed roots. Though it was a fantastic sight to behold, Pushkin felt naught but dread in its presence and resented Indrik for bringing him there. Even so, Indrik approached the tree with Pushkin still sitting in the saddle. Pushkin, having his fill, dismounted his horse, and then nearly stumbled upon the fungal growths blanketing the soil in capped masses. Indrik knelt down and quickly proceeded to eat the mushrooms that formed along the trunk and infested the forest floor around it.

"Indrik, no! What are you doing? This is lunacy." Pushkin forcefully grasped the horse's head and a made a powerful, but futile attempt to pull Indrik's head away from the mushrooms. Indrik responded with a great and gruff snort, jumped back and with a mighty stomp to the ground, knocked his master a meter backwards.

"Indrik."

Pushkin, dazed by the fall, watched as his horse devoured the blue-capped fungi with an obsessed fury. His eyes widened at the sight; Indrik's once nut-brown coat and mane paled and became a shimmering white in just a few short moments. Pushkin, not wanting to lose his closest ally to whatever atrocities this accursed tree was producing, once again made the attempt to dissuade the powerful beast. Again he was thrown back and nearly trampled. He could only watch, with the threat of tears forming in his eyes.

"Damn you!" Pushkin rushed the steed once more, if only to tackle it to the ground, but as his body met with powerful impact into Indrik's side, he was merely halted. The horse threw himself with a great scream, head down into the man, lifted him off of his feet and threw him several meters. Pushkin was knocked unconscious with the forceful landing.

Kirill Pushkin awoke to gentle nudges to his face and arm. Opening his eyes he found Indrik staring over him with great blue eyes, from a head and body that appeared to have grown immensely in both size and ambiguity in what he perceived to have been only minutes of unconsciousness. Just above Indrik's eyes centered on his now strange head, a single horn expanded with authority towards the sky.

Kirill stood and looked to the ground. None of the mushrooms could be seen; Indrik, he figured with his heart nearly sinking into his stomach, must have consumed them all. He allowed his eyes to follow the ground to the tree's trunk, only to find the tree too had changed. It was quickly dying; no longer white, instead nearly black and completely bare of leaves on what remained of withered and dead limbs. Kirill looked to the stallion once more and found no malice in the benevolent eyes staring back at him, and somehow found the familiarity once more. It was Indrik, his old friend, however transformed, it was still he.

Kirill couldn't secure his thoughts around any of this and stood for a moment, dumbfounded. As he stood, staring down at the dry forest floor, in his peripheral vision he could see a great darkness emptying out of the forest surrounding them. He turned his head upward to watch as hundreds of the three-legged creatures, rushing in some great stampede and weaving between the trees, quickly bore down upon him and Indrik.

That he should die in such a way, completely bewildered, knowing nothing of the world he had once thought to surround him, he nearly fell to his knees. Indrik stirred quickly behind him, and Kirill turned to see the mighty horse rear in a powerful stance and let out a sound he had never before heard. It echoed through the trees and traversed in determined ferocity along the forest floor, blasting the ears of all who heard it. Indrik, with a force far greater than that used to throw Kirill, trampled down onto the tree, uprooting it from the soil and throwing it back into a raucous fall to the ground. Kirill swiveled his head around, awestruck at the sight of hundreds of these dark, mutated beasts falling lifelessly to the forest floor. What he had seen could never find an explanation and what it meant, Kirill could never fully understand, but he didn't care. Instead, a great sense of relief had swept over him, as if the death of the tree and the foul beasts of the forest meant that all of this had ended.

Once his stupor had subsided, Kirill realized he could no longer feel the pain in his stomach. Though a warmth remained, if was no longer what he had once felt from the accursed tree. Instead, he felt the warmth of the sun was piercing through breaking clouds in a forgiving sky. It was already a new day, and the first in some time that was free of the horrible storm.

A final ride returned Kirill to the town, which in the light of day, he had not seen for some time. It looked to be in shambles. Kirill dismounted and walked with Indrik to his brother's and entered without knocking, to find Dominika and her children collecting and disposing of the meat he had only just given them.

"Oh, Kirill. You startled us. I'm sorry. We have to dispose of the meat as it is beginning to smell very foul, and somehow, though we didn't notice yesterday, as I'm sure you didn't, the meat is already rotting. That must've been the cause of Nyekev's illness."

"I am so sorry Dominika. I'm afraid I provided the entire town with tainted meat. I was desperate, and it was all I had. I fear I may have cursed Nyekev and the others to—"

"Please, do not trouble yourself. These have been trying times for all of us, and Nyekev has improved greatly since last you visited. He left only minutes ago to speak to the town. He believes that now, as the storm has lifted, some of the men may be able to set out for Kurmynsk and we may finally receive assistance. He was looking for you as well. He knew that you and Indrik would be the first to volunteer."

Kirill exited the elder Pushkin's home, both relieved and puzzled. It was almost as if the past few days had not occurred. Surely, he would assist, but how would he explain the change in Indrik, and what of Vladimir and his family? Kirill looked around just outside of the house for Indrik, but he could not find his horse. He managed to find only hoof prints leading back alongside the tracks they had left moments before. Kirill followed them for nearly an hour before accepting that Indrik had departed deep into the forest and that somehow this was as it should have been. He could never have explained a great white, horned stallion to a town full of people who he had given tainted meat and nearly killed.

Kirill wandered back to town with numerous thoughts zipping through his mind, with not one that he could manage to grasp firmly and force to find a place within reason. As his brother was dispatching nearly the entire town to do whatever deed he required of them, Kirill approached with a somber presence. Nyekev greeted his younger brother with endearment and apparent for-giveness for the tainted provisions. Kirill suspected Nyekev and the others must have felt much like him; healthy and relieved at the breaking of the storm. However, Kirill could only partially main-tain such relief as he shared with it the great burden of knowledge. In this, he maintained concern for Vladimir and his family, none of which were present.

"Come brother, we've a great and busy day before us."

Kirill grasped his brother in a mighty embrace and nearly wept at the sight of such recovery.

"It is good to see you in such great health Nyekev. But…"

Kirill decided it best to discuss Vladimir immediately and allow what remained of the disconcerting occurrences to fall to the past, regardless of what Nyekev's response may be. The catharsis was needed, and he had grown weary of deception.

"I visited Vladimir and his family yesterday afternoon…"

Kirill awaited his brother's response.

"Did you? I'm sorry to say you have been the last to see them alive."

"How do you mean, brother?"

"Did you not hear the thunderous sounds last night?"

Kirill heard the sound of the blizzard, the sound of the stam-peding creatures of horror, and the sound of a great majestic beast commanding the heavens before felling a wicked tree. He suspected none of these were the sounds to which his brother was referring.

"I heard a sound, but I thought it the storm."

"It was the fall of the mountain, Kirill. I'm fearful Vladimir, Mila and their family, were buried with their house. The mountain must have become too encumbered with the snow, and as the storm reached its pinnacle, the land gave way and buried the foothills."

Kirill thought, and with it the remnants of that horrible curse.

"Kirill, I should also tell you, your meat is tainted. It was splen-did and succulent when first we had it, but Dominika had found it rotting earlier today. Thankfully, it seems I suffered the worst of it. Such is the burden of the mayor I suppose."

Nyekev laughed heartily and patted his brother's back.

"Don't look so down, brother. I think we've seen the worst of it. By the way, where is Indrik? I don't think I've ever seen you without that horse."

Kirill had explained, giving into deception once more; Indrik had fled that night, possibly startled by the sounds of the mountain, and quietly received his brother's sympathy knowing that he could not accept it.

That day the town gathered what little provisions remained and divided them evenly, giving more to the three men sent to seek help. Kirill was included, though he refused the additional provisions and insisted the other men take the greater portion of his share. Even so, he and the others survived the venture and returned with a cow, a bull, a horse, some feed, seeds, a few vegetables and even fuel for Nyekev's old truck. It was a scarce, but greatly appreciated gift; one that they would eventually return, as Rubstoyevka recovered slowly, but surely over the next few years. It would meet and overcome further adversity from time to time, with the comfort in knowing that having survived the great storm, little else could so vastly impact their lives. Deciding that one day he may tell his brother the truth of Rubstoyevka's struggles, Kirill accepted that as life and strength were finally being renewed in the town, it was best he leave the past buried, and carry the burden of such knowledge alone for the time being.

Indrik was never seen again, but Kirill alone knew that the great burden Indrik beared for the town of Rubstoyevka warranted whatever freedom the beast desired and likely ensured a future befitting only the greatest of beasts.

Indrik

(Russian: *Индрик-зверь,* **transliteration:** *Indrik zver'*)
in Russian folklore, a fantastic beast, the lord of all animals or beasts ruling atop the mythical 'Holy' or 'Saints' mountain where no other foot may tread.

It was believed that as the Indrik walked or stirred, the Earth would tremor and quake.

The word 'Indrik' is derived from the Russian word 'edinorog' meaning unicorn, as the Indrik is described as a gigantic bull-like beast, roughly the size of an elephant, with the legs of a deer, the head of a horse and a single enormous horn protruding from its snout.

PHOENIX

So many men keep falling,
Their feet can't touch the ground.
We can hear them calling,
Their voices make no sound.

Along ethereal paths,
Float as they drag the chain,
And we can hear them pass,
We can almost feel their pain.

Eyes set upon this fire,
As the flames reach the sky.
Behold costly desire,
And hear the voices cry.

An ocean made to rise,
Bodies now flood the Earth,
And where no city lies,
May we soon prove our worth.

Though we're left in this wake,
Only to carry on.
A future we've to stake,
A past to build upon.

Sheltered between the stones,
We save all that we can.
With this water; atone,
And with these words we plan.

AEH 10-23

It was a night in late October of 1892, and like many of the nights preceding and the several sure to follow suit, it presented a frigid air and slow-moving breezes bearing the contempt of all those unfortunate to suffer them. Of these, a young man, Leif, lies upon the small bed perched in the darkest corner of his somber cabin, covered with few meager furs and a small quilt too old and too carelessly kept to present much shield to the night. As a rule, Leif slept lightly. It was one of the many aspects of life to which he had become accustomed since taking refuge in the quaint two-windowed cabin located deep within the pine woods he called home.

A trapper by trade, he kept very few luxuries and the most valuable item to be found in his possession would be his rifle. He kept this in close proximity at all times. A rough life, but one which suited him far better than any found amongst other people, of which he had very little preference. Cold nights alone, surrounded by the only world he knew well enough to claim as his dominion, were a bittersweet comfort.

His greatest gripe would be the glass work encompassing one of the windows, which insisted upon being particularly troublesome during such wind-swept nights. The razor thin slit in its easternmost side, allowed even the slightest breeze to moan and whisper through defeating any silence suitable for deep sleep. On this particular night, however, the breeze seemed to carry with it, an ominous and startling sound. It began quietly as a wailing, indiscernible in its nature, but clearly panicked. It started low in tone, but sounded as if it were growing in vocals as it heightened in pitch and volume. Leif, with recently opened eyes, could feel his skin crawl beneath his covers. It seemed unnatural, and certainly cause for alarm. A noticeable contradiction to the normal low toned wails of the wind, and as the seconds turned to minutes, it contin- ued to grow and peal until it became something more uniform and singularly identifiable; a gut-wrenching scream.

Slightly startled, Leif rose from his insignificant slumber and peered through the window opposite his bed. He could see little in the moonlight, but waited for a short period, staring into the dis- tance with great fixation. After a few moments, as his eyes adjusted to the lack of light, it revealed minor details through the windows low visibility. Somewhere in the distance, almost due north from Leif's cabin, could be seen a faint light flickering and swaying al- most in synch with the rising and falling screeches. Leif was the only resident in these woods, save for one other; an old hermit living similarly in solitude nearly one mile to the north—the very same area from which the light and screams seemed to originate.

Having met this man once, Leif made great effort never to again unless it simply could not be avoided. The elderly man was uniquely disturbing in his mannerisms and visibly obsessed, telling of deep, unsettling desires through the stern focus in his sharp, listless eyes. Upon immediate first impressions at their first and only encounter, a great sense of unease became permanently embedded within Leif. In the back of his mind he had somehow expected to eventually hear screams emanating from the strange, elderly hermit's cabin.

Leif quickly clambered through his cabin and threw on his trousers and trench-coat, adjusted his suspenders, and stepped into his worn boots. He made no attempt to acquire his lantern, as it had expended its last bit of allocated oil for the night, and opted to rely on his familiarity with the woods to support a possible need for stealth. However, before exiting the cabin, he retrieved his rifle propped against the wall. Should any danger present itself, advan- tage attained in the obscurity of darkness would be taken in vain without the range of offense permitted by his rifle. It was a tool with which Leif was commendably skilled, even in the shadows of night.

As he stepped out of the cabin onto the darkened earth to start his short trek of investigation, suddenly the screaming ended, in a dead silence. Leif proceeded around the cabin and saw that the light too had dissipated with the wail. He considered for a moment returning to his cabin bed and trying once more to initiate the previously unattainable slumber, but knew that it would likely be impossible, with his calm state so thoroughly dashed. Instead, he walked into the woods making an attempt to follow in the general assumed direction where once the light could be seen.

The gleam captured in his sights, as he peered down his barrel to the north, was brief and would do little to serve his aim. In response, he licks he fingers and massages them around the sight. Should need be, he would be at the ready with the glimmer of moonlight.

Given the presence of the mountain foothills, just over one mile north of his cabin, Leif assumed the light to have originated at a nearer proximity, based on its perceived height. Though likely a short distance, Leif knew it would be best to make haste. He walked quickly, but carefully through the darkness. Fortunately, Leif's familiarity with the near two hundred acres of the surrounding forest was profound. Imprinted in considerable detail with great care in his mind, the plot could be travelled blindly without Leif losing his way. Not a foolish man, Leif understood that the woods could still pose unpredictable dangers with its teeming nocturnal wildlife. He found it a blessing that on this night, the light of the moon had provided just enough illumination. Leif could clearly see every nook and cranny passed through and passed by.

After some time spent traversing through the varied terrain, Leif believed he was closing in on the old man's cabin. Mere minutes passed with further trekking until he had caught sight of the homestead. It was strikingly similar to his; he had never noticed how exact the similarities were, and in fact, he questioned himself on whether he had taken the right path or turned around somehow.

He knew this cabin could not be his. The surrounding terrain was slightly different, with the foothills and a small stream near and the forest growth appeared thicker.

Once within few feet from the cabin, Leif halted. It most certainly was not his cabin. One clearly defining difference positioned in the doorway of the cabin exclaimed with grand ambition; *this is the old man's cabin*. Or rather, it was. For in the doorway, the body of the old man lay stationary in a pool of black blood which cradled the soft moonlight.

Leif readied his rifle and positioned it at his shoulder as he continued towards the body, crouching slightly and heightening his awareness. In the low light of the moon, he crept cautiously and with great care spent in keeping his own shadow from obscuring the lifeless body as he fixated upon it, watching for any slight movement.

Standing just over the clearly deceased body, Leif leaned down at its side and made an effort to examine what remained of the old man. After looking down upon the corpse only briefly, he made a great effort to force composure throughout his body as he could feel it recoiling and trying desperately to leap backwards, retreating into the woods. The corpse before his was on its back, revealing a faceless head and a morbid display of flesh, gleaming with streams of blood coursing through and around the curves of worn, misshapen, muscular tissue. Remnants of bone once comfortably hidden within the skin now cascaded with a collection of supportive tissue showed through with gnarled detail. These segments of bone seemed to sink back into the skull as if fearful of their introduction into the external world. Any structural integrity once available to the aged head was fading quickly and leaving only ghastly ruins.

Leif momentarily removed his view from the skull and instead allowed his eyes to canvas the entire scene and collect all details that may help explain the grisly preceding which led to the old man's unfortunate demise. Once again, as if beckoned, his sight focused upon the head and traced around the outer edges of the would-be face, and just before the ears and temples he spotted it; a chilling realization. The skin had been ripped clean from the face by some forceful hand with deeply digging fingers. The areas where a face had once been attached were a testament to the incredible strength used to create such shreds, tears and ghastly indentations. There was something else though, accompanying the tortured imagery of a missing face—the eyes. They too were missing, leaving only sockets emptying into the darkness of a lifeless skull. Leif walked slowly around the body with great care applied to avoiding foot placement too close to the remains, including those detached from the man for whom Leif can now only take pity. Still surveying the alarming scene with no small amount of morbid curiosity, Leif identifies, just beside the head, the man's eyes, or rather, their vestiges. The eyes appeared to be halved hemispheres missing the crucial retinas, irises, and lenses. Hollowed in the center, in Leif's mind, these seemingly chewed whites of eyes bore a grotesque and absurd resemblance to a pair of large fish eggs after large bites had been subtracted. If only Leif could grasp how unfortunately apt this horrible comparison would prove to be after closer inspection. Leif retrieved the fleshy remnants of eye and turning them gently in the moonlight revealed precise cuts in the soft sclera surface produced by the strange razor teeth that had bitten into them. Leif replaced the organic debris beside the body and briefly struggled to keep his mind from forming reenactments of the occurrence.

Slowly, but with light-footed precision, Leif stepped over the body and entered the cabin. It was dark and with the small traces of moonlight allowed to pass through the window, Leif could see very little. Straining his vision, he peered into the space near the cabin's front door and could make out the glimmer of shapely glass—a lantern. Leif retrieved the lantern and returned to the exterior of the cabin as he twisted free the remaining wick and removed the glass casing. Using his last match, he lit the lantern and returned to the cabin entrance.

Stopped in the doorway, Leif marveled at the strange sight before him. The cabin, now wholly unique in comparison to his own, was filled with many unidentifiable trinkets and mechanical objects in various states of construction; disrepair and in some cases, decay. Most of these items of apparently clever design, appeared to be lacking in various ways and were clearly unfinished. Of the great array of machines, tools, equipment, and scientific instruments, nearly all were scattered violently across the room, which itself bellowed in its remarkable state of disarray.

It was made clear to Leif that a struggle had recently ripped violently through the cabin and must have been enacted by something vast and powerful, if only briefly, to somehow end with the death of the old man. Taking care to watch his step, Leif in curiosity, searched the homestead for further indications of the preceding, and surveyed the many unusual items assembled around him in disheveled madness.

Mechanical constructs of a wide variety; some made to look like and probably function in ways similar to various animals, some with purposes entirely alien to Leif, and still others appearing to function in more serviceable means. Of the latter, Leif recognized what appeared to be a sort of adding machine seemingly designed to manage complex calculations, a machine similar to a phonograph connected to an array of wires which led to large magnetic structures carved into recesses in the walls, and another familiar device closely resembling a phonetic telegraph. Leif stood amazed and bewildered, slowly absorbing the wonders around him.

He continued forward, trekking deeper into the cabin. Suddenly, his attention was beckoned to the northwestern corner of the room; a small, cluttered desk. Sitting atop the desk, supported by countless scattered papers scrawled with a lifetime of research, Leif noticed two incredibly small, semi-spherical and lens-shaped pieces of glass gleaming in the light of the lantern. Leif gently rotated one of the glass pieces between his fingers, feeling the smooth surface as he leaned forward to take a closer look. Leif leaned into the desk peering into the lens and focused upon the displaced and distorted view of the wall before him, and with this movement, the side of his head was caressed with the leathery touch of what he immediately identified as human skin.

Quickly, Leif turned to meet the bearer, only to find a face, hanging from a large metal hook which protruded through a hole in the left side where the eye typically would be found. The featureless and disembodied tissue hung with a slackened and weary expression. It was very pale, and appeared to have been coated with a fine dust or ash. Touching the skin, Leif realized it wasn't human. Instead, it appeared to be a combination of leather and bare, treated rabbit hide, cobbled together in a grotesque amalgamation meant to resemble a human face. Leif pulled it from the hook and turned the face in his hands to view the concaved backside. He held it up to the lantern and noticed etchings in the inside right cheek. The etchings appeared to be a random collection of numbers and letters followed by a series of several indiscernible markings. Those characters Leif could identify appeared to read 'AEH 10-23-EFC'. If these markings weren't random, Leif couldn't begin to guess as to what they meant.

Continuing his search, Leif proceeded to the front of the cabin, just before the largest window. He found other remnants of manufactured skins among copper and iron plates welded into familiar shapes; body parts. The machinery was fashioned together with the very distinct resemblance of an arm, a leg, and the upper portion of a torso, and they too, bore etchings, sharing only the first three letters, 'AEH'. Kneeling down with the lantern in hand, he allowed the light to crawl inside the torso piece. He couldn't completely understand the sight hidden within the piece. He knew he had never seen a more complex arrangement of incredibly minute gears, locks, and shafts. These were joined with wires, filaments and fuses, also remarkably small, and unique to anything Leif had ever perceived.

Leif, still facing the window, rose to his feet, and in the darkened distance, he could see a bright light beam through the trees, positioned directly across from the front of the cabin. The light flickered rapidly; gaining intensity until the flickering gained such

quick uniformity that it appeared to become one solid and constant ray of bright white. As feverishly as the blinding light shined,
another scream pealed in and grew in equal intensity until reaching
almost deafening effects. Soon the light appeared to become dim
and the screeching softened in some strange paradox, as though
they reduced; the fading of sound and light seemed to somehow
imply their source was growing closer to the cabin. Leif couldn't
quite understand the phenomenon, but he knew it to be certain;
though the light diminished in brightness, it grew in radius and the
sound, though dampening in pitch, grew more defined in audibili-
ty. As the light and sound grew in proximity, Leif could identify a
contour in the glow of the light.

Both tall and large, presenting the silhouette of a grossly dis-
proportioned human figure with a light radiating from its chest,
the figure stood perfectly motionless before the cabin. Leif's skin
began to crawl along his backside and scalp as he lifted his rifle and
peered once more through the sight. He began to identify every
frightening detail with his intense focus.

This was no man; it was a machine. Some sort of automaton
constructed of copper and steel, clothed in portions with various treated hides in what appeared to be an attempt to make the
creature more visually comparable to a human. This attempted
illusion was clearly a failure and no person with clear sight would
mistake the behemoth for a human. In addition, the immediately
discernible peculiarities of the figure, a large ball of light shone
brightly, floating unattached in a hollow center of the chest. The
arms hung at the sides, supported by a system of gears, chains
and wires, similar to that seen in the torso piece. The legs, planted
firmly in the ground, were awkwardly proportioned, as the base of
each was unusually large and appeared to encase what must have
been massive inner workings stemming from the lower torso.

Though wholly inhuman, the machined mockery was wearing
a face Leif recognized as human skin; it belonged to the old man.
Still gleaming with the remnants of the lifeblood and tissue once

used by the natural bearer, the machines face was shielded with a mask of its creator.

Leif squeezed the trigger and shot, as the rifle kicked into his shoulder he looked over the sight to watch the body fall. Only it didn't. It stood perfectly still and he could hear the bullets fruitlessly ricochet.

Suddenly, the mechanical being began to scream as the ball of light in its chest began to grow and radiate with a brightness competing that of the sun. Leif turned away to stare into the dark cabin and allow his eyes to regain vision in the darkness. His body quaked as he worried deeply, immediately regretting leaving the safety of his own cabin. He closed his eyes and opened them, batting his lids frantically towards the floor of the cabin, quickly trying to plot some kind of escape. The machine had been several feet away; he may yet have the option to simply flee.

Leif turned back to the window, only to meet face to face with the sentient machine standing just on the other side.

In one swift, liquid and surprisingly organic movement, the machine curled its hand and fingers around Leif's rifle barrel, squeezed it shut, ripping it from Leif's hand, and then flinging it backwards into the woods. Leif became immediately aware of the machine's unearthly power as he had almost fell forward with his rifle. He wanted desperately to flee, to duck and cower, or even shield himself in futility with his own arms, but he could do no such thing. He stood stiffly, experiencing a greater state of panic than he had known himself capable. As the machine's hand returned to its side, it stared into Leif's eyes and Leif returned the locked glance. He could see two small, glassy and moistened circular wedges resting in the center of the machine's spherical eye pieces. As they reflected the moonlight, he could identify them as lenses; natural lenses from natural eyes—human eyes.

In an instant, the machine swung its hands forward and stopped them both at either side of Leif's head. The machine screamed and blasted blinding light from its chest before Leif even had a chance to react. Leif, for a split second, could feel a pressure on the temples of his head, followed with a shooting pain which echoed and repeated through all sides of his head as they seemed to contract and converge. Within his remaining conscious moment, Leif watched as the blinding bright white turned to black and listened as the deafening scream turned to a muffled sound of broken shards and intense drowning pressure, before all became silent.

As the light dimmed and retreated into the machine's chest, Leif's body revealed itself as a motionless carcass on the floor, surrounded by broken fragments of bone and punctured flesh decorated with blood and limp cerebral tissue. Among dozens of scattered, fragmented pieces, two large sections of skull meshed and intersected together were lightly supported with what little muscle tissue and skin remained attached to Leif's neck.

The machine returned its hands to its side and turned away from the cabin. It retreated back into the obscurity of the woods with several large and hurried steps; leaving behind the deceased stranger, its creator, and the home from which it was born. The large automaton travelled with the fervor of one looking to leave a troubled past behind. A new life was quickly given into the woods, and with it, came the sacrifice of two previous lives.

For several aimless miles the machine traveled quickly, proceeding with the bright radiance in its center, lighting the way. Several hours later, the machine's beam became the only light in the forest, as the moon crept behind a mass of dark and heavy clouds, as if it wished to refrain from participating any further in the night's proceedings.

It began to rain and clinks echoed through the trees as the drops began pelting the machine's body. Still the being continued to travel to an unknown destination, slowing progressively as the rain hit the ball of light in its chest which hissed and steamed maliciously in response to the cold assault.

This attack from the heavens was not in vain, as the waterfall took its toll on the lighted sphere and it began to fade quickly and dissolve. The machine rapidly declined in speed and after a few

minutes with the decay of the sphere, the machine halted completely and collapsed to the forest floor.

The woods grew darker and the rain heavier as the storm
picked up, no longer lighted by the newborn intruder. The deluge
faded and was replaced with thunder and lightning. A fire born
of lightning grew from the east, and only slightly hindered by the
recent rain, it travelled quickly through the entire forest until the
trees and foliage were bathed in a sea of flames. Hundreds of acres
of land were scorched and destroyed, leaving only charred remains
and rubble.

The area became lush and wooded once more after several
years passed, and with time it was settled once more. A town was
eventually established upon a few acres of cleared land. The remnants of the two cabins and their owners were mostly lost to the
unforgiving nature of time, leaving only rubble and shards which
were simply displaced and forgotten. The town grew rapidly as
more and more settled in to prosper in the rich depository of metals mined from the surrounding earth and the woods were further
cleared for the expansion.

On a brisk July morning, a small group of miners, while shov-
eling a few heaps of top soil, witnessed a faint glow obscured by
the dirt and mulch. Were it not for their excited pursuit of precious
earthly metals, they might have let it be...

...but a scream, bellowing through the town that morning declared the unearthing of a horror.

THIS PARTICULAR BIRD

This particular bird.

Maybe it wasn't a bird,
It wasn't immediately identifiable.
It came from the heavens,
Perhaps a gift not meant to be named.
A beauty in voice, a profound poise,
Assured it's form was inconsequential.
In fact, we all, in this gathering,
Myself among other beasts,
We seemed to become formless.

We had been restless wanderers,
But in this bird's timbre we'd halted.
We, once arrested by our routines,
Once sickened with our worries,
Once incapacitated by our fears,
Once overwhelmed with our burdens.
All seemed to fade away,
To retreat into some forgotten past,
Held at bay by a shrine of notes.

If only for a brief collection of moments,
Spent ensnared by perfect harmony,
In this forest clearing we were carefree.
As we were suspended in space and time,
We heard nothing but song.
Our minds emptied and filled with voice.
Our highs and lows caressed by tone,
And blessed by an aural divinity.
Life composed in range and pitch.

Surrounded in a soft cadence,
We wild were made tame.
As song we were given,
Of this particular bird.